Hotel D

THE SHAHS

NIKA STONE

Hearthound Press

Join My Newsletter

For bonus scenes, previews, updates and tea-based shenanigans, sign up for my newsletter:

https://nikastonewrites.com/stay-in-touch/

Stay With Me

Aesha

I really don't belong here.

Technically, on paper, I do. I have an invitation, courtesy of my bossy younger sister. But this hotel that I find myself in, with its marble floors and lush antique carpets and two-story tall floral arrangements, is *so* not my speed. This place's energy says *Relax. Enjoy the luxury. Be still.*

My energy? It's more like *Wipe the cheese doodle dust off of your shirt before you get it on the fancy hotel's leather couch.*

In my defense, I came straight here from work, and the cheese doodles were the only dinner I could scrounge up from the depths of my desk. Longingly, I think of the sexy, sexy ribeye I *should* be having with my best friends and my sister Mala right now. That was the birthday celebration *I* wanted. But Mala talked them all into going in together for one big present, which turned out to be a ticket for this event hosted by Ria Black, lifestyle guru extraordinaire. Mal even agreed to "watch" my son (and by "watch" she meant "completely spoil") for the weekend so that I could be here.

The brochure for "Operation-Help-Aesha-Calm-the-Fuck-Down," as my sister dubbed it, promised that a weekend spent in this luxurious hotel with Ria and her team would be "rejuvenating" and "transformative." I can't argue about the fact that I need some downtime; the last few months at my firm have been insane. Because of that insanity, I got here late and missed the hors d'oeuvres. As hungry as I am now, I'd settle for transforming this invitation into a bag of airline peanuts.

I snag a glass of something cold and bubbly from one of the adorable young assistants milling around the room. At least there's still liquor.

The crowd settles into our assigned seats as Ria Black takes the stage. She's gorgeous and polished, perfectly lit by a single spotlight. The glow emphasizes the perfection of her tight chignon, her swanlike neck, and her form-fitting red gown.

"Ladies and gentlemen, welcome to the Hotel d'Amour — and welcome to the Weekend Escape."

I bet Ria Black is always presentable. I bet her stockings never rip and her hair always behaves and her clothes fit correctly and she wakes up looking just. like. this.

I don't even own a pair of stockings anymore, and when I wake up, my hair is a literal tragedy.

"Tonight," Ria announces from the stage, "I invite you to open yourselves up to connection." The crowd murmurs enthusiastically.

"Now, this work isn't easy. It's difficult to shift so much in a few short days. But if you'll make the effort, the rewards will be extraordinary. So be prepared. We're going to ask you to open your minds," she says. "To open your hearts. To open your — well, whatever else you open is up to you."

I nearly choke on my champagne as the audience laughs. What the heck was that supposed to mean? Nobody better be opening anything next to me. I need some clarity on what this event is about.

"But enough preamble. Let's start making these connections. If you'll look under your seats," Ria says, "you'll find a numbered bag with your essentials for this evening. Let's get those out now."

I do as I'm told. When I reach for the bag, I'm surprised. Instead of the fancy paper creation I expected, I find a gorgeous locally-made leather clutch in a deep jade.

It's the kind of thing I'd lust after but would never buy. Oh, I'd visit it in the purse section of Nordstrom's, multiple times. I'd stop and stare, then give the buttery leather a few strokes before I put it away in favor of yet another sensible black bag. And then, if I was lucky, my sister would get sick of me being so ruthlessly practical and buy it for me.

I am somehow reassured by the appearance of this little beauty. No matter what else happens tonight, at least I got a cute accessory out of it.

There's a handwritten tag attached to the clutch. It has the number 523 written on it. The same as my ticket for this event. I flip it over, looking for some kind of direction, but the back side is blank. I try to find one of the youthful assistants. They've put away their trays of champagne — a pity — and are all helping other confused patrons.

I'm wondering if it's not too late to sneak out and go for that steak when the great lady herself finds me.

"Aesha, isn't it?" She's just as pretty up close. Her brown skin glows with warmth and a subtle touch of bronzer. I think we wear the same shade. I wonder if she does her own makeup.

"Aesha Shah, yes," I say. How did she know it was me? There are at least a hundred people in this ballroom. Did Mala send them my photo? She must have.

"I'm Ria. It's lovely to meet you in person." Wow. Even her eyeshadow coordinates with her gown. I see why Mala likes this woman: she's basically her clone.

I want to be as put together as Ria Black when I grow up. Although I wonder if I'll ever manage that milestone. At this point — turning 43 today and still eating cheese doodles for dinner — that ship may have sailed.

Despite all this buzzing in my head, I give Ria my best professional smile and shake her hand.

"I wanted to meet you since your registration for the weekend was submitted by someone else," she tells me. "I expect you're not as familiar with my work as most of the folks here."

"My sister is a big fan of yours," I reply. I don't mention that I will most likely be kicking said sister's butt later.

"That's lovely to hear, thank you," she says graciously. "I hope you enjoy the experience. Normally I require that everyone sign up for themselves, but her letter was so sincere. It touched me. She convinced me that she knew you well enough that we could keep this a surprise."

Great. I hate surprises. Definitely kicking my sister in the shins.

"I'm not sure what experience I'm supposed to be having, frankly. She was light on the details."

"That's on purpose," Ria says. "I prefer it when guests come into the weekend without preconceived notions about how it's going to go."

"Sure, sure. However, I would love more info than that. What exactly is this event supposed to accomplish?"

"The Escape isn't supposed to be anything in particular," she tells me in that soothing voice of hers. "It's more about the opportunity to take a pause from the busyness of life.

"That pause is to help you learn about who you are now — and who you need to become for the next phase of your journey. In some cases, it's also to help you find the person or people who can help you help you get there."

Okay, yeah. That bucket load of vagueness will not do. If I'm giving up my weekend for this, I'm going to need a lot more detail.

I'm about to ask Ria if I can at least get a copy of the agenda when one of her assistants approaches. A tall-ish, dark-haired man follows close behind.

"RB?" I suppress a sarcastic snort. Maybe I should make my

assistant call me by my initials. "We're nearly finished with the matches. This gentleman hasn't found his just yet."

The man holds up a tag. It reads 523, just like mine. Interesting.

"Thank you, Tara," Ria says. She glances between the man and me. "Excuse us a moment?"

While the two of them confer, I discretely take a good look at Mister 523.

There's a lot to look at. He's tall. Lithe. I know that's the kind of description you only find in books, but it suits him. The gray slacks and jacket he wears can't hide his lean, muscular build. He looks like a swimmer. His tan skin suggests that a lot of the swimming happens outside.

I wonder where he's been. Portland's been in the rainy season for months now.

Then I notice his glasses. Those chunky black frames are a hipster stereotype, but somehow, they absolutely work for him. Their thickness makes his bright brown eyes and long, delicate lashes stand out even more.

I take another sip of champagne and force myself to turn away. I shouldn't be so obviously checking him out. But my eyes fly back to him like a magnet. Especially to his mouth.

His closely trimmed beard and longish hair are more pepper than salt. He's probably my age or close to it. His soft-looking lips make me think of filthy, dirty things I have no business thinking.

Calm down, woman, I tell myself. But there's That Hair. Yes, it deserves the caps. The touch of gray at the temples, the unruly curls just waiting for someone to run their fingers through them — it should be a crime for any man's hair to be this gorgeous. He's tamed it with some product, but I can tell those curls have a mind of their own.

Curly-haired boys have always been my weakness.

I set my glass down on a nearby table. It must be the champagne. Alcohol plus lack of food has got me loopy and horny. I'd better find some food after this, or I'm heading straight to bad decision land.

Ria touches my shoulder, bringing me back to the real world. Heat rises in my cheeks. I might as well be one of those old cartoon characters with their tongue hanging out, hearts for eyes, and a flock of birds chirping around my head.

"I'm excited for you both to meet each other," Ria declares. "So 523 A? Meet 523 B."

I holds out a hand. "Hi. I'm —"

"Hold on, please." Ria interrupts. I blink at her in confusion.

"You might've missed the announcement before. At these events, we don't start off sharing our names."

Yep. Definite hippie vibes.

"I know that might feel unusual," she continues. "But remember: The point of this experience is an escape. Not just from your everyday life, but also social convention. Therefore, while you two are partnered for this exercise, I'd like you to remain anonymous. Is that okay?"

I feel my eyebrows jump up to my hairline. Really wondering what kind of hippie weirdness my sister signed me up for. Is this some sort of weird sex cult? I swear, if it's a weird sex cult, I'm not just kicking Mala's ass — I'm telling our mother.

Although with this guy, I might do the sex part first. He looks like he might have some skills in that area. Then I'll snitch.

"Fine with me." His voice is a rumbling bass that makes my entire body tingle.

"Sure." I shrug. "YOLO, right?" Good grief. I am so uncool. No one says YOLO anymore.

He smiles at me, and my heart actually skips a beat. I decide I don't care who says what, as long as there's a chance I will get to climb this man like a tree.

"I appreciate the both of you being open to that. I think it bodes well for your night." She hands us a keycard. "Your workspace is here. For you two, I recommend Exercise Five to start. Enjoy your journey."

Ria gently pats us both on the shoulder and disappears, the delicate scent of vanilla in her wake. The man — is he A or B? Does it matter? — and I exchange an awkward smile as Tara says, "Follow me, please."

In for a penny, in for a pound, I guess. Goodness knows I could use a pounding.

Okay, Aesha. Shut that down now. You're an attractive woman. You are not so desperate that you have to jump on the nearest available dick. No matter how sexy a package it arrives in.

Stepping into the elevator with the two of them, I decide I'm going to make the most of this experience. Whatever it turns out to be.

Theo

She's really nervous.

She's trying not to show it, but the way she keeps wringing her hands and smoothing her hair makes her tension obvious.

I hope this doesn't make me a shitty person, but seeing her jitters makes me feel better. I'm not exactly at ease myself — it's reassuring that it isn't just me.

She checks her reflection and smooths her hair again. I fight the urge to do the same. These shiny surfaces in the elevator are making me self-conscious, too. Guess that's something else we have in common.

Her hair is perfect. It's dark, a little wavy, and cropped just above her shoulders. The golden streaks around her face sparkle, matching the amber in her soft brown eyes.

Soft is the perfect adjective for her. Not her outfit; it's the opposite. Her crisp white shirt makes her skin glow, and the severe navy suit with matching glasses gives off a hot as hell sexy librarian vibe. Did not know I was into that, but all of a sudden, I am one hundred percent for it.

But I can tell that underneath the stern clothes, her figure is lush. Curvy. Soft in all the right ways. I imagine what it would be like to lie next to her. To touch and taste her. To come home to her.

Whoa. Dial it back, Theo. That's a lot of expectation to put on a woman who hasn't even said ten words to you yet.

We exit the elevator on the fifth floor.

Tara gestures to the right. "Your room is just down this hall. Remember, you'll try Exercise Five first, and see what kind of breakthrough it leads to for y'all. You can use any of the others as you please."

Tara pats us on the shoulders the same way Ria did — I guess neither of us is hiding our nerves as much as we think — and tells us to have fun. That the space is ours for as long as we need it.

My new partner and I head to the room in silence.

I should say something. I keep sneaking looks at her, trying not to stare like a creepy asshole. Mostly I'm freaking out. I haven't had such an intense reaction to a woman since April —

I shut down the thought. *None of that, brain.* Not tonight.

We reach the room. She takes out the key card and stares at it for a minute. I can almost hear the pep talk she's giving herself. I get it. This whole setup is weird as shit.

"Hey." She looks up at me, brown eyes wide. I want to stare into them, to get lost in those tiger's eye depths, but again — trying to minimize the creep factor. I give her arm a light touch instead.

"I know we signed up for it, but — we don't have to do this. If you're not comfortable, or if you'd rather go get a drink at the bar, or head back to our rooms and forget the whole thing altogether, that's fine with me." My brain chants *please, please, please* in a steady rhythm. I'm not sure which option it wants more.

Her face lights up with the most perfect smile. She gives my hand a squeeze.

"Thank you," she says. Her voice holds genuine relief. "That's sweet of you. Really, I'm fine. I want to try this."

She opens the door to an enormous suite. The walls and furnishings are luxurious, plush. Their rich colors and dark-stained woods offer a cheerful antidote to the bleak weather outside. The door to the bedroom is ajar. I try not to notice the massive king-sized bed inside.

We drop our bags on the old-fashioned wooden table in the center of the living room. Now that we're alone here, the brief moment of bravery outside the door has transformed into intense awkwardness. I spy the fridge and pull out two bottles of water. She accepts one; I think she's as grateful for something to do as I am.

I'm fascinated by the contrast of her dark cherry mouth and the white glass, and the way her throat moves with every swallow. My own throat is suddenly dry. I take a quick swig of my drink.

"Shall we?" she says. She seems determined.

"Right down to business. I like that."

"No sense dicking around, as it were."

I nearly choke on the water I'm drinking. Trust me to make an awkward situation even more so by practically killing myself. She walks toward me, concern on her face, but I wave her off and excuse myself to the restroom. A few awkward coughs later, it's all over.

"Everything okay?" she asks when I return.

I nod. "The only thing hurt is my pride. It can probably stand the blow."

"Sorry. I'll try to keep any other folksy sayings on the PG side." The saucy sparkle in her eyes belies her words.

"Why limit yourself? I'm willing to risk it if you are," I reply. She gifts me another one of those stunning smiles. I can't wait to make her do it again.

"Okay, let's see." She opens a white mailing envelope labeled with the number five. Inside are two blindfolds and a small piece of card stock. She skims it, a frown flickering across her face. She hands the card to me.

Exercise 5.

Both partners should place themselves in a comfortable position.

Put the blindfolds on if you're feeling shy.

Then ask your partner: Why are you here?

Well, shit.

I look up at my new partner, sure that my face bears the same confused expression she wore moments ago. I flip the card over, but the reverse side is empty.

"That'll teach me. I should've taken you up on the drink in the bar option," she says.

Her voice is somewhere between a laugh and a sob.

"Still on the table," I offer. She shakes her head no.

"I'm gonna need something stronger than this water, though." She roots around in the mini fridge, and cheers when she pulls out two tiny charcuterie boards and little bottles of Prosecco.

"Snacks first. Then the baring of souls can begin."

"Maybe we could work up to it while we eat?" I suggest. "Share a few basic facts so we aren't going in totally blind?"

She nods. "I'd like that."

She sets out the trays, and we dig in. I learn that her favorite color is green, that she loves churros, and that she talks with her hands. Her favorite childhood memories are of watching Bolly-wood movies with her mom and siblings. She takes her coffee black with a pinch of salt and cinnamon.

Other things I learn: her perfume smells like jasmine and rain-water. Her voice gets a sexy little rasp when she's been talking for a while. And when she takes off her jacket, she stretches like a cat, with total abandon. It's the sexiest thing I've seen in years.

In the face of her warmth and openness, it's easy to share.

I tell her I've always wanted a blue house, but not just any blue: it's a very specific shade somewhere between teal and navy, and I'll know it when I see it. That I unironically love my hometown of Mountain View, and despite five years in SoCal, living there was not for me.

She wrinkles her nose in the most adorable way when I confess my love for Tallegio cheese. She protests because it smells like gym socks, and is appalled when I agree but admit I still love it. I get a satisfied "I knew it!" when I say I was captain of the swim team, and a swoon when I disclose that I love baseball because it meant spending a Sunday afternoon with my dad.

The meal is over too soon. I'm pretty sure I could talk with her for hours. I *want* to talk with her for hours. Instead, we tidy up the table. If our hands touch as we clean up, or her shoulder brushes mine, or we look in each other's eyes a moment too long, it doesn't mean anything. So I tell myself. I don't want to assume. But I think she's into me, too.

I really, really hope she is.

When we finish our task, she gulps the last of her wine. Puts her hands on her hips. The action pushes her breasts out in this way that makes me want... shit, it just makes me *want*. I'm so turned on I can't think what I would do first.

"All right," she says. Her voice is a touch thicker from the alcohol. "Let's go."

"Do you want —?" I wave a blindfold in her direction.

She laughs as she takes it from my hands. "Oh, God, yes."

I'd like to hear her say that in other circumstances. Very, very naked circumstances.

She claims one end of the love seat; I take the other. I slip on my blindfold. The black satin is smooth and cool against my eyelids. She takes a deep breath, holds it, releases it. I do the same.

"Ladies first," I offer. My heartbeat speeds up. The sensation seems to echo through my whole body.

"There are no ladies in this room, sir," she says with a husky laugh.

"We can pretend."

"Ooh, role play. A little early for that, aren't we?"

"Is it ever too early for the handsome stable boy and the lady of the house to sneak off for, um, riding lessons?"

"Nope. Never."

I laugh. Damn. I *like* this woman.

"So. Why am I here?" Her voice sounds the way silk feels sliding across my skin. "What do you suppose it means? Like, why am I in this town?"

"Sure. Start with that."

"I was born and raised in Beaverton." I can almost hear her shrug. "It's just west of the city. I didn't love living in the burbs. It's fine, but it's not for me. I'm a city girl. I like being able to walk to the grocery store, or the pharmacy, or whatever. So I moved into Portland proper as soon as I grew up and could afford it. You?"

"Job transfer. I'm a principal."

"Huh." My shoulders tense. Maybe she has capital-O Opinions about education.

"I don't know what that means."

"I just don't know any principals," she replies. I relax. "All my friends are lawyers. Little kids or big?"

"Middle school."

She laughs. "Oh, my. You are a glutton for punishment."

"You're not the first one to make that observation." April always said the same thing. My throat tightens. I close and lock that away.

"I like the job, even though middle schoolers can be... shark-like. We do our best to teach them how not to eat each other up."

"Between social media and all the raging hormones... Good luck with that."

"Just call me Sisyphus." She laughs again, and I'm ridiculously pleased. Tolerating nerdy jokes is a good sign. Actually laughing at them is another level of awesome. Especially the way she laughs, like her whole body is in on the joke.

"So we're done, then?" she asks. "That seems almost too easy."

She sounds uncertain. Maybe a little tense.

I could say yes. We could shake hands, part ways, and just be done. But that's not how this is supposed to go. It's not how I want it to go. I need more time with her.

"From what I've read of Ria's work," I say, my tone gentle, "the whole point is to go beyond the superficial. I don't think we're there yet."

Her sigh holds a resigned quality. "I was afraid of that."

"If you're feeling uncomfortable—"

"No, I just — my sister signed me up for this. It was a birthday present. She always wants me to go wild and let my hair down."

"And that's not something you do?"

"Oldest child syndrome. I wouldn't even know how." Her voice is quiet. Thoughtful.

"This whole thing — I don't get the point, and these directions are so vague — I feel out of control. It, rather. *It* feels out of control. In a bad way."

She cuts herself off, but her tone makes it clear: Out of control is dangerous territory.

Still, I wonder if it isn't precisely where she needs to go.

"If it was up to me," she continues, "I'd be down the street at that Argentinian steak place."

I go along with the change of subject. "Sounds great. I love those little cheese breads —"

"Pão de quejo, yes! They're so fucking good," she moans. To hell with the cheese breads. It's the noise she made that sounds so fucking good.

Stop being such a horn dog, I tell myself. I fail spectacularly.

"All right, sir. I told you mine," she says. "So tell me yours."

Shit. I swallow, trying to get past the lump in my throat. I do not want to go there right now. Not with her. But I don't have a choice. Time to be brave.

"My best friend encouraged me to attend. Direct quote: 'It's been five years. You've been lonely long enough.'" My voice is ragged. I don't trust myself to say more.

She reaches for my hand, gives it a squeeze. I squeeze back and hang on to her.

"My wife... It was cancer, and it was brutal. I missed her — miss her — every day."

"Fuck. I'm so sorry," she murmurs. I squeeze her hand again. Her skin is soft. I draw circles on her palm with my thumb. Her thigh presses against mine.

"I'm — I really am as okay as I can be. Therapy, grief counseling, the whole nine yards. And time helped, of course."

"So you're in a better place these days?" she asks.

"I'm better," I agree. "And I came because I realized Sean was right. I have been — I am lonely. And I don't want to be anymore."

Aesha

The ache in his voice is so raw. It breaks my heart. I want to rip off my blindfold and pull him close.

"I get that," I say instead. "The loneliness. That hollow feeling in your chest, like your heart's been snatched out and replaced with a block of ice."

He lets out a long, shaky breath. Settles in to the seat. "Did you lose someone, too?"

"Not in the same way." I do not want to talk about my divorce. Not with the first man who's interested me in forever and a half.

"What happened?" Ugh. That voice of his. So gentle and warm and disarming. I bet his students love talking to him. I bet they pour their little hearts out because he listens so thoroughly.

"Nothing special. Just two lawyers trying to build careers and a marriage at the same time. The careers lasted. The marriage didn't." I put a hand to my throat, as if I can physically push the shame of it back down into my body. Thank goodness for this blindfold.

"Vikram and I got the world's greatest kid out of it, though. So it wasn't a complete disaster."

"Breakups happen," he says. He's rubbing soft, slow circles on the backs of my hands and I am fucking dying. His touch is so gentle. I want him to touch me like that all over.

"That's not something to be embarrassed about." He continues tracing those maddening circles on my hands. My core is pulsing in time with each stroke.

"In my head, I understand that," I say. My voice cracks. He has to know what he's doing to me. Has to. "My heart, though. It's having a harder time learning that lesson."

"You'll get there. You're smart, funny, sexy... How could anyone resist you?"

I gasp a little when his lips graze my knuckles.

"Is that okay?" he says, concern in his voice.

I nod vigorously before I remember he can't see me. "Oh, yes. That is okay. That is way more than okay."

He laughs at the eagerness in my voice. I couldn't care less. I'm so damn turned on my whole body is practically vibrating. As long as he keeps touching me, he can laugh all he likes.

And touch me he does. He lifts each finger of my right hand, planting a gentle kiss on the pads. When he repeats the gesture with my left hand, I stroke his beard with my right. It's softer than I expect. He leans into the caress.

"I —" he huffs out a laugh. "This is unexpected. I don't even know your name."

"Does that matter?" I say. I'm surprised by how little I care. "There's a reason we aren't supposed to share those, right?"

"But how do I ask if I can kiss you if I don't know it?"

"I think you just did." I can't keep the smile out of my voice. He's good, this one.

"And you didn't answer." He pulls me up and off of the loveseat. That gentle tug brings me so close that every inch of me is pressed up against every inch of him. The layers of fabric between us do nothing to stop the blaze of heat between our bodies. Nor can they hide the thickness of his arousal, insistently pressing against me.

"May I?" That whisper in my ear makes my knees weak. I cling to him like he's a life raft and I just fell off of the Titanic.

"The list of things I want you to do to me only starts with kissing," I confess.

"Is that right?" He nips my earlobe, immediately soothing the sharp sensation with a kiss in the same spot. It's so hot. How is that hot? I don't understand why it makes me want to rip off my clothes and ride him like a bronco, but it absolutely does.

He kisses me again, this time just below my ear. "Tell me what else you want."

"I want —" I can't hold back a moan when his lips graze my throat.

"What?" His thumb brushes across my lips, soft as velvet. I take it all the way into my mouth, swirling around it with my tongue. He hisses, like he couldn't hold it in even if he tried.

"Gods, woman, say it." His voice is tight. As if it's causing him physical pain not to give me exactly what I'm craving this very instant. "Tell me what you need."

"I want... to let go." My words come out in a rush. "I — every day, I'm responsible for so much, I just — I need not to be, for a little while."

His mouth comes down on mine, and every other thought evaporates.

I thought I'd been kissed before, but nothing has ever felt like this.

He tortures me with gentle passes of his lips over mine. Over and over, he deliberately grazes my mouth, feather light, darting in for a sip and away again like a hummingbird. The faint tickle is almost painful. I sigh with relief when he brings his mouth down on mine firmly, beguiling and demanding all at once.

I lean into the tart champagne taste of him. He takes his time, seducing me over and over with every lick and thrust of his tongue.

I'm overwhelmed by the softness of his lips, the harsh rasp of his beard, the roughness of his hands on my cheeks. I sink into every single sensation and willingly drown.

This close, I can tell how good he smells — like cedar and citrus and something deeper, an earthier scent that makes me want to bite him. I need to know if he smells like this all over.

He breaks off the kiss, leaving us both breathless and panting. Our foreheads meet, as if our bodies can't bear it unless some part of us is touching.

"Here's what's going to happen." The commanding tone in his voice thrills me right down to my core. "I'm going to take off my blindfold. I'm going to leave yours on. And then I'm going to lead you over to that bed."

I shiver as he strokes my collarbones. Jesus, how am I this horny? It's like I've never done this before.

"Your job is to tell me what you like. I don't need much. Yes. No. Faster. More. Understood?"

I nod. Just in case he's still blindfolded, I add, "Yes."

"Good. Now my job is to show you how to come, as many times and as many ways as I can manage it.

"Lucky for you," he murmurs, "I'm an excellent teacher."

He leads me into the bedroom, walking me backwards until my calves hit the edge of the mattress.

He unbuttons my blouse, taking his time, kissing each bit of skin that's revealed as my top falls away. The zipper makes a scritchy metallic sound as he slides my skirt off, taking his sweet time. The fabric whispers down my hips, tracing the path of the fabric with his hands, leaving me in just bra, thong and high heels.

The air stirs around me, chilling my skin. I turn my head towards the sound of his footsteps as he circles me in a leisurely way.

"Fuck," he whispers. His voice is close. "You are perfect. I could look at you forever."

"Please don't," I beg. I might die if he doesn't get inside me soon.

He laughs, low and sexy, then kisses me so hard I can't breathe. It's perfect.

He lays me down on the bed, still kissing me as if his life depended on it. He breaks away to nip at my neck, swirling open-mouthed kisses down its length, before he makes his way to my breasts.

"Fucking magnificent," he says with awe in his voice. He grazes my nipples with open palms. Even with my bra still on, every touch is like a hotline to my clit. I can't hold back a moan as he bites my left nipple through the fabric, licking and sucking it to soothe the sting.

He gives the other breast the same treatment. I clench my thighs together, desperately seeking relief.

I plunge my hands into his hair, luxuriating in the soft curls. He lets me, for a moment. Then he grabs my hands and pins them over my head.

"Oh, no," he corrects. I hear the slide of fabric against fabric, and then cool silk drapes across my wrists. He lets me go only to make a quick and sturdy knot.

"I'm in charge right now, remember?" he reminds me. "So let me be in charge. Let me give you what you asked for, sweet."

I make a needy noise somewhere between a moan and a whine. He swallows it with another one of those heady, drugging kisses until I settle down. I'm so wrapped up in what his mouth is doing to mine, I don't even notice when he strips me bare.

His hands and mouth tease my skin with long, tender strokes. I can't tell where he'll touch next. A kiss on this ankle. A slow stroke on the back of that knee. A bite on the inside of my thigh. I'm out of my mind and nearly ready to come from this alone.

When he finally, finally puts his mouth on my pussy, I almost jump out of my skin. It's too much and just enough. He's relentless, gripping my ass with both hands to lock me in place while he licks every bit of me with that marvelous, talented tongue.

I am lost in a haze of *yes* and *please* and *more fuck yes more.* When he sucks my clit into his mouth, I come so hard I see stars.

He slides behind me, wrapping me in his arms and holding me tight as aftershocks hit me, one after the other. The crisp cotton of his shirt cools my overheated skin. Eventually, I come down to earth, helped along by his soothing murmurs in my ear and the delicious citrus scent of him and the delicate circles he draws on my back with his palm. When I turn my head to kiss him, I taste myself on his lips.

I press my ass into his lap, feeling the length of him through the layers of cloth between us. He groans, breaking away from our kiss.

"You want more?" he teases.

"I want it all," I demand. I've never meant anything more.

He takes my bound hands in his own. "Then give me something to look at," he demands.

He makes me spread myself open with one hand. My skin is hot with embarrassment and lust. I don't understand how he's turning me into this shameless woman, so eager to let him see all of me. I open my legs wider and he swears under his breath.

"So fucking hot," he says. I shake when he makes me finger myself with the other hand. This is who I am now. A woman who shamelessly displays herself for her partner's pleasure. Who boldly slips her fingers into her own pussy and revels in the effect it has on him. I feel like a fucking goddess.

The rustle of clothes being shed and the sharp rip of a condom wrapper catch my ear. Then the mattress sinks a little under his weight, and his bare skin slides on mine as he slips behind me. We both moan at the contact. It feels — he feels — so fucking delicious.

He teases me at first, stroking my folds with his cock before slipping inside slowly, so slowly, an inch at a time. I thrust my ass back, demanding more, and he takes the hint, thrusting in all the way to the hilt. It's perfect. He's perfect. I tighten around him, drawing a groan from his throat.

"Fuck! You feel so damned good." He emphasizes every word with a thrust.

He's holding on by a thread, I can tell. I want him to let go, too. I'm dying to feel him lose control like I am.

The slap of our bodies coming together again and again makes me dizzy with lust. I'm so, so close. His hand on top of mine adds just the right amount of pressure and soon I'm shaking, gasping, coming again with a shout, my voice somewhere between a scream and a sob.

He speeds up his thrusts, like he's been holding back this whole time, waiting for me and now he can let go. I lean into him as his entire body tenses; he growls in my ear as he comes. I've never heard a sound so wonderful in all my life.

We collapse in a sweaty heap, lying quietly, limbs still tangled together. My mind is perfectly blank. I'm content to lie still as he unties my hands, leaving a trail of kisses on my wrists as he frees me. He removes my blindfold, teasing my overheated breasts with the cool slide of satin and the rough skin of his fingertips until I'm restless and yearning for him again. This time, I get to run my hands through those glorious curls, all over his taut abs and smooth skin. When he slides inside me he holds my gaze the entire time. We're skin to skin and as close as we could ever be, but that look strips me to the bone. It demands that I give him everything, that I hold absolutely nothing back. It's almost a relief when we both come again and can break the contact.

After a while longer, we separate long enough for a quick rinse in the suite's enormous shower. When we make it back to the bed, we hold each other for a little while, trading lazy kisses and talking about nothing in particular.

Just before we fall asleep, he looks down at me, eyes warm with satisfaction.

"By the way, it's Theo."

"Aesha," I reply, blushing.

Somehow, after everything else, this exchange feels the most intimate of all.

Sleeping with someone new is strange.

Figuring out whose limbs go where, who gets which blankets, how much touching each of you likes — all that takes some adjustments as you go. It's been years since I had to think about someone else's comfort.

But Aesha and I naturally fell into a comfortable position, as if we'd been doing this for years. Our bodies just fit perfectly together. I got the best sleep of my life. I try not to read too much into that.

Of course, we didn't get all *that* much sleep. After all, I had to keep my promise of making her come as many times as I could. She didn't seem to mind one bit. Not when there were so many surfaces to explore, and so many ways to use them as leverage. I can't decide which was my favorite: the loveseat or the shower. I think we'll have to give both another shot just to be sure.

Eventually, our grumbling stomachs forced us to leave the suite. Somehow, we stopped touching each other long enough to visit our individual rooms for a change of clothes. She's still in hers when I head down to the hotel's restaurant and grab a table for us.

First things first: I text my friend Sean. I can admit I was...

surly when he suggested this event to me. No way would a weekend self-help retreat fix my lonely state. I did everything except tell him to shut the hell up — and that's only because we've been friends for fifteen years. I knew he meant well.

Then last night happened.

Aesha rocked my entire world. Not just with her body — although her body is absolutely spectacular — but her entire being. Her brains, her determination to try this even though it was clear she'd rather be anywhere else: I couldn't have picked someone more perfect for me if I tried.

I've heard other people met someone at one of these events. It always sounded too good to be true. But I'm man enough to admit that I was wrong, so I tell Sean the truth. This conference was exactly what I needed. I laugh out loud when he demands proof that it's really me sending this message. Smart ass.

I'm sipping coffee and reading the news on my phone when Tara, one of Ria's assistants, approaches.

"Good afternoon, Theo," she says. I return the greeting. "Ria asked that I follow up with you and your partner for Friday's exercise. We'd love to know how your evening went."

Just at that moment, Aesha enters the restaurant. She walks across the room like she owns it. I'm mesmerized. That cream-colored sweater dress makes her skin luminous. And the way it hugs every one of her curves makes me want to throw her over my shoulder and carry her back upstairs.

I have to laugh at myself: I've got it bad. I'm not even a tiny bit ashamed.

"Hey, stranger," she says, nodding at Tara. "May I join you?"

"Ooh, are we playing this game again?" I ask. "I've always wanted to be a sexy international spy."

She laughs out loud, and my heart swells a little. "I like who you are just fine, Theo."

Tara takes all of this in with an amused grin. Working with Ria, I'm sure she's seen this all before.

"So things went well then, last night?" Tara asks. Aesha and I share a look. A slight flush rises in her cheeks. It makes her even more beautiful.

"The exercise was, um, fruitful, yes," she says. I nearly inhale coffee through my nose.

"It was great. Really... opened up several avenues of exploration for us both," I add.

Her smile becomes a full-fledged grin. "I'll be sure to share that with Ria."

Tara thanks us for our time before walking away. We try to remain serious, but one look at each other and we're both cracking up.

"Fruitful?" I ask, handing her a cup.

She shrugs. "Should I have said stimulating? Scintillating? Provocative?" The way she whispers that last one in my ear does indecent things to me.

"Point taken." I hold up my hands in surrender.

"Thank you. I like a man who knows when I'm right."

A server stops by our table, and we order lunch. Sandwiches or something. I'm only half paying attention to anything that isn't Aesha. Her hair is swept back in a slick bun, making those gorgeous amber eyes stand out even more. She's done something simple with her makeup that gives her a lovely glow. Or maybe that's just the way she looks when she's been well-satisfied. The thought certainly isn't doing my ego any harm.

"Penny for your thoughts?" Rather than admit my vanity, I decide to pivot.

"We've skipped a lot of the usual get-to-know you part," I point out. "Tell me some more of that stuff."

"Like my job, that kind of thing?" She sounds almost surprised. I want to know everything about her. I can't imagine anyone not wanting the same. Nobody could be that foolish.

"I do employment law. Plaintiff's side," she answers with a shrug. "Making sure folks get what they're entitled to is my jam."

"That sounds complex."

"It is." She takes a big sip of coffee. "But that's the fun bit."

"What's the hardest part?"

She thinks for a second, her brown eyes glazing over a little. "Sometimes, there's a big difference between what's right and what's legal. That can be pretty discouraging."

"Does that stop you?"

"Never," she scoffs. "It makes me fight twice as hard."

"So what you're saying is that you're a badass."

"Basically. I don't lose very often."

Her confidence knocks my socks off. I bet she doesn't lose. A vision of her coming home all full of adrenaline after she's kicked some wrongdoer's ass flashes through my mind. I'm waiting there, ready to help her work it all out.

Huh. My brain keeps circling back to the idea of her and home. If I had any sense, that would make me nervous. Instead, it feels like the greatest thought that's ever been thunk.

"So you, Theo." Her query interrupts my musing. "What's the day-to-day life of a principal like?"

"I've only been here for a couple of months, so I've spent a lot of time getting to know the district. Other than that, the job's the same as it is everywhere: solving the problem of how to do too much work with too little money. But I can't imagine doing anything else."

"Persistent. I respect that."

"It's like you said. That's the fun bit." The smile she gives me makes me feel ten feet tall.

After lunch, we attend a meditation session. I meditate all the time, but today, I completely fail. It's almost embarrassing. How am I supposed to concentrate on the teacher's instructions when the curve of Aesha's waist is right there for the touching? When the jasmine and rain scent of her is driving me to distraction? The only thing I need to contemplate is how soon I can get this woman naked again.

Post meditation, we wander into one of the conference rooms. There's a wellness fair, complete with demonstrations and local service providers. We take a quick perusal of the aisles, but there's nothing that draws us in. Before we leave, I make sure to stop at one of the resource tables. I slip a few lists and some business cards into my pockets.

"What's that?" Aesha asks. I hand her a postcard. She tucks it into her purse.

"Lists of local support groups, psychiatrists, therapists."

"For?"

"Sometimes students and parents need help. Since I'm not local, it's nice to have resources like this available for folks who need it. Maybe your clients need it too."

"You're a good man, Theo." She kisses me on the cheek. "Now tell me: how do you feel about playing hooky for the rest of the day?" she asks. That mischievous sparkle is back in her eyes.

"What'll we do instead?" I waggle my eyebrows suggestively. She rolls her eyes.

"You're still pretty new here, right? Let me be your tour guide."

"I can't think of anything I'd like more."

It's true. Until she takes me to a pirate bar.

That's not a joke. I'm skeptical, right up until I realize I get to play pirate-themed mini golf under black lights. It's so weird, I can't resist. Aesha trounces me, of course. Her victory dance is so awkward and terrible, though, I'd lose all over again just to watch it.

We stumble back out into the daylight, blinking awkwardly, and walk down to the riverfront. She points out landmarks: the Japanese Memorial, the old paddle steamer, Skidmore Fountain, and tells me about their history. I listen, I really do, but on the inside, my heart's glowing like a neon sign. This woman is here with me. She wants to be with me. I'd pinch myself, but if it is a dream, waking up is the last thing I want to do.

Once or twice, I take her hand as we walk. She tolerates it for approximately two point five seconds before giving me a quick squeeze and letting me go. Noted: PDA isn't her thing. I can work with that.

By the time we're done with our walk, there's just enough light left for us to take silly selfies with the elephant statues in the Park Blocks. Then we hit up the elegantly old school El Gaucho and have the best steak of our lives.

It's so good, in fact, that the only thing we can do is head back to the hotel to burn those calories right off.

We stumble into my suite, wrapped around each other. Knowing that my taking charge gives her extra pleasure, I come up behind her and slide my hand underneath her dress.

She sucks in a breath as my palm glides over her ass. I lightly snap the waistband of her thong.

"Take these off. Now," I order. Aesha shivers, but she also obeys.

Reaching around her body, I undo the buttons at her neckline, leaving the sweater open and exposing her bra. Her nipples are already pebbling into tight peaks. She makes a needy little sound as I pinch them through the lace.

"Again?" she whispers. "Please?" I roll them between my thumbs and index fingers, pulling just a touch. Aesha grinds her ass into me, making my already hard cock throb. I nip at her neck and slip two fingers inside her. She clenches around my fingers. I massage her clit with my thumb, which makes her cry out.

"Fuck, that's so good." Her hips thrust back and forth as she fucks herself on my hand. I keep up the pressure on her clit. She's close: I can feel it. I twist my fingers inside her, and she shatters around them. It's the most beautiful sight I've ever seen.

"Get over the desk," I say.

She makes her way to the old-fashioned wooden surface and obediently bends over it while I deal with my pants and grab a condom. I need to be inside her now. She's adjusting her position, spreading her legs apart when I slide inside her. I might die from sheer relief.

I thrust into her, reveling in her slick, soft heat. All I can hear is the slap of our bodies as she arches back to meet me.

"Look in the mirror," I demand. Her eyes darken and her mouth parts as we watch me fuck her, watch her fucking me back. I pull one of her hands off of the desk and place it firmly over her clit. She takes the hint and strokes herself slowly. My cock gets even harder watching her. I pull her hair, and she hisses out a curse.

I tighten my hold on her hips as my orgasm builds. Aesha's fingers dance faster and faster, until she comes again on a deep sob. I thrust once, twice, and the third time I come so hard I feel it in my spine.

We clean up quickly and settle into the king-sized bed. She nestles into my arms in that weirdly perfect way. We hold one another, drifting between not quite asleep and barely awake. The last thought I remember thinking before we drift off to sleep is I could fall in love with this girl.

In the morning, I reach for Aesha before my eyes are even open. It's the last day of the event. We should probably attend another session, just so we can have something to tell our friends, but this private moment between us is something special. I need more of that first.

God, Sean's gonna give me all kinds of shit. I already know he'll hold this over my head for years. I can't wait for these two to meet —

My brain stutters as I spot the envelope with my name on it resting on the nightstand. The stationery looks thick, luxurious. I don't want to disturb it. I want to go back to five minutes ago when I was planning a future with her. Not looking at the end of all my hopes.

I open the letter, admiring her softly rounded script, and let her break my heart.

· · ·

Theo,

This weekend was... I don't have the words to say how extraordinary I found it.

I was hoping for a pleasant distraction and got so, so much more.

Alas, the real world demands my attention, so back into the fray I go.

I will cherish the memories of this time, and of you.

Thank you for being the most wonderful surprise.

A.

~

$$\mathcal{A}esha$$

"**S**hit. I'm gonna be late," I complain to my sister. I keep cruising the school parking lot, desperately searching for a spot.

"You can't be late, Aesha." Her voice is a carbon copy of our mother's, even distorted through my car's speakers. "You'll look like an asshole in front of all the other parents."

"Thank you, Queen of the Obvious, for that brilliant observation."

"I'm just saying. How will you find a hot single dad if you show up late to all the places that they are?"

"It's parents' night at the elementary school, Mala. Not speed dating at the bar."

"Could be a from little column A, a little from column B, if you do it right, sis."

I snort. Only my sister would try to turn the least sexy activity ever into an opportunity to troll for dates.

"I am not looking for a man."

"Mmm. Still hung up on the hot guy from the hotel?"

"Whoops, it's time to go. Love you! Bye!" I chirp, disconnecting the call.

I'd given Mala a highly edited version of that weekend, but she was smart enough to read between the lines. She was disappointed, however, when I made it clear that there was no sense in talking about (or thinking about, or dreaming about) Theo. That ship sailed a month ago when I snuck out of his hotel room without leaving my number.

Mostly, she was impressed that I let myself relax enough to take a chance on a hot guy.

It hadn't felt like taking a chance, though. It just felt... right.

This lot is packed. I guess a lot of other parents made New Year's resolutions not to suck, too. After parking a block and a half away, I run back to the school. I make it just before the lights dim and find a seat in the back of the auditorium/gymnasium.

Now that Mala's brought up my time with 'the hotel guy,' as she calls him, I can't get Theo or those two days off of my mind. Even this mad dash into the school reminds me of rushing out of my office after work to get to the Weekend Escape. Worse, I can't eat those stupid cheese doodles without getting all up in my feelings.

The middle school band comes out. I scan their shining, nervous faces. As always, my heart lights up when I spot my sweet boy. At eleven, Riz is just barely bigger than his tuba, but he loves playing that ridiculous thing. It makes him happy, and although it means I practically own stock in earplugs, his happiness is mine.

When Riz sees me, I get a slight nod before he turns back to talk to the girl playing trumpet next to him. Now that he's a tween, he's too cool for the frantic wave and giant smiles that used to make me ache with fierce mama love. These days, it's more subtle. Watching the tension leave his face after he spots me confirms that he's happy that I made it tonight. It's different, navigating this phase of his life, but it's still pretty darned good. I'll take it.

The kids play with only a little more enthusiasm than talent.

They've gotten so much better since the music teacher came on full-time. I send a quick video to Vikram, my ex, and his parents. Riz' Dada and Dadi will be bragging to all of their friends about their talented grandson for at least a week.

The band finishes up with Stevie Wonder's "Sir Duke," and we parents give them a standing ovation. Riz bows over and over along with his classmates, dark hair flopping in his face. He clearly loves this. Because Mom's work is never done, I make a note on my phone to schedule a haircut for him.

As the band students shuffle off to seats on the other side of the auditorium, Principal Saunders takes the stage.

"Welcome, parents." She offers a warm smile to the crowd. "I'll try to keep this brief. I know you're not here to listen to me talk.

"We are so happy to show off the extraordinary work your students have done over the previous term and to help them think about where their art is headed as we start the next. Creating inspired, well-rounded learners has always been and always will be the heart of our mission.

"That said, I know some of you have concerns about funding issues. Not just here at our school, but in the greater district. As my colleague says, it's that age-old problem of too much to do and not enough money with which to do it."

I'm only half-listening, but that phrase catches my ear. I haven't heard anyone say that since —

"In order to address this, a group of our schools has formed a task force. I invited the leader of that group to talk about what our fiscal future looks like — and what our community's parents can do to help. Please welcome Langdon School Principal Theo Kearney."

My heart speeds up. It's got to be a coincidence. I'm sure there's more than one man with that name who works in education. This couldn't possibly be my Theo.

It is.

His hair's a little longer, and his beard's thicker, but I'd know him anywhere. Heat rises under my skin as he takes the stage. My breath catches in my throat as he starts to speak, the low rumble of his voice setting off fireworks in my gut.

I don't hear a word he says. I'm too busy remembering how it felt to have that lean swimmer's body over me, his weight pressing me into the mattress, shaping me into someone new. Someone who responded only to the rasp of his beard on my thighs, the dark thrill of his voice ordering me to put my body in his hands, the taste of our last kiss.

Him whispering "I could fall in love with you" as he fell asleep.

I had to walk away. That intensity... It was way too hard and way too fast. That's not me.

I am the queen of moderation. The girl who always keeps her cool. But moderation doesn't exist when it comes to Theo. I needed to escape his orbit before I let him ruin my carefully planned life. I frantically text my sister.

> Hotel guy is here!

She writes back immediately.

> Good! Now stop being such a commitment
> phobe and get him back.

Oh, Mala. As if it were that easy. Even if I thought a relationship between us could make sense, even if it weren't all hot and heavy and scary fast, how would that even work? How could I glide past the awkward explanations? How could I convince him to take me back? Or at least to take me back to bed? As if I want that.

Jesus, I want that.

I startle when the other parents in the audience offer him a round of applause, and belatedly join in. I'm sure it was great. Everyone rises from their seats, scattering to the different classrooms to check out all the students' work.

I follow them, still in a daze. How am I going to get through this evening? What do you say to the lover you abandoned with a breezy note and not even a backward glance? I don't know the etiquette for this situation. Maybe I can avoid him for the rest of the night.

But of course, it takes me a while to slip through the crowd and get over to the area where the band students sit. And of course when I get there, Theo's talking earnestly with Riz. Just my fucking luck. I watch them for a moment, this boy I adore and this man I want too much for my own good.

My son talks with his whole body, gesturing intently at something or other on his instrument. His hands fly as he draws pictures in the air to stress his points.

And then there's Theo. Who, bless his heart, listens to Riz with full attention. I swoon like a debutante.

He was like that with me, too. I've never known anyone like Theo. He has such a genuine eagerness to listen to what people have to say. It was incredibly seductive for me as a full-grown woman; my sweet little boy has no chance. I watch him blossom in real time under the fullness of Theo's regard, and my heart stings with a longing I don't dare to voice.

Then Riz sees me.

"Hey, Mom! Guess what? Mr. Kearney plays the tuba, too!" Riz gives me a great big smile, which I can't help but return, regardless of my pounding heart and shaking knees.

Theo turns to face me. I see his polite expression slip as he recognizes me. Selfishly, I'm glad to know this moment shakes him, too. Although he quickly gets his professional mask back up, those blazing brown eyes roil like a stormy night sky.

"Ms. Shah." He offers a hand. "Nice to see you." His palm is warm and supple, the opposite of my dry, cold one. Inwardly, I cringe. I would forget my lotion today of all days. Ugh.

"Mr. Kearney." I keep my words clipped, tight. Riz rolls his eyes a little. He knows when I'm putting on my lawyer voice. "Sharing some good tips, I hope?"

"Getting some, actually. Riz has very solid technique. I hope he keeps up with his lessons."

"Mmm," I say, desperate to escape this conversation. I look down at my boy, who puffs his chest out like a tiny pigeon with pride at being singled out.

"Hey, beta. Are you ready to show me all the cool stuff you made last term?"

Riz nods. "Just gotta clean my mouthpiece and put away my instrument. I'll be back in ten minutes, okay?"

He's gone before I can even agree. I watch the door long after he passes through it. Anything to avoid meeting Theo's eyes again. My tongue is glued to the roof of my mouth. He deserves a proper explanation instead of this completely awkward silence, but I can't seem to stop staring at the floor.

"I didn't think I'd see you again," he says.

"Same," I manage. "But — we should talk —"

He holds up a hand to stop me. "No need. I'll be discreet about our previous encounter. I'm sure you'll be as well. Consider it water under the bridge."

Oh. Okay then.

"Um. Thank you?"

His smile is polite. Impersonal. "Don't mention it."

Not sure what I expected. Or why my feelings are hurt. I'm being ridiculous. This is the best outcome I could hope for.

"I hope you'll be part of the committee?" he asks, breaking another awkward silence. "We could use someone with your skills and connections."

Committee? What committee? Oh, crap. I was so lost in my memories of our time together that I wasn't paying attention at all.

"Sure," I hear myself say. "I'd be happy to help." As soon as I figure out what the hell we're talking about.

"Excellent. Thank you for that." He pulls out his phone and hands it to me. "I'll need your number and your email, please."

"Of course." I input my contact info with hands that only

shake a little. "There you go. That's my work cell and office email. Oh, let me add my personal —"

"That won't be necessary." The frost in his voice cools my jets. "Work contacts are more than sufficient. I'll add you to the email chain. We've got a lot of work to do."

He turns to walk away. I can't let him go. Not like this.

"Theo — I —"

"I have to get going, Ms. Shah." He gestures at the crowd. "I need as many folks as I can muster to support the committee."

"I see. Of course," I say, picking up the shreds of my dignity.

"It was great to see you again. I look forward to your help with our project."

"Me too, Mr. Kearney."

It feels like a punch to the gut, but this time, I let him go.

Memories flash through my mind again, but the reality of this last interaction makes them bitter. He wants to treat me like any other parent. As if our weekend meant nothing to him. As if he hadn't held me down and fucked me until I couldn't see straight. As if he hadn't threatened to love me.

You walked away from him first, Aesha, my brain helpfully reminds me. Stupid brain.

But it's true. I chose to walk away.

It's only now that I realize that was the biggest mistake of my life.

Theo

Crap.

I just made the biggest mistake of my life.

Why did I invite Aesha to join my project?

The way she left made it clear she wanted a clean break between us. I respected that. It hurt like hell, but I left it alone. Could I have found her? Sure. With the information I had, it would've been a simple thing to search the state bar's website and get her details. But I flatter myself that I'm self-aware enough to read the room, and stalking has never been my style.

Which is why this ache in my chest galls me. All it took was one minute back in her presence, and I'm a lovesick puppy. No amount of willpower or good intentions could stand up to those gold-flecked eyes and stunning curves. I want — no, I need to be close to her, in any way I can. Consequences be damned.

So I asked her to be part of the fundraising team. I know it was a bad idea. But she said yes. Even though her face said she'd rather be anywhere else on earth than talking to me, she said yes. It means she doesn't hate me, at least. I hold on to that like a raft.

This event is a great one — showing the parents the art their kids are creating encourages them to sponsor the budgets for these teachers — but I barely pay attention to any of it now. I smile and nod at the parents and shake hands and hand out business cards to at least a dozen people whose names I immediately forget.

How am I supposed to concentrate? The woman I hoped would be mine forever is walking around here, nonchalantly breaking my heart all over again.

After an hour of glad-handing parents and staff here, I'm fried. I find Patricia Saunders and make my excuses. As I head to my car, I text my friend Sean.

Meet me at SD. Urgent.

Be there in twenty, he replies.

My brain goes on autopilot while I make my way to Swan Dive. It's a downtown bar, but not in that sleek, wood-paneled way. It's more like your older brother's apartment: a little grungy, there's probably something growing in the kitchen, but it's kombucha, so don't freak out. They'll let you in with jeans, because Portland, but they might judge you if you don't at least consider a local brew. But it's got great food and bartenders who pour generously, so fair tradeoff.

When Sean walks in, I amuse myself by watching the number of heads that turn and how many not-so-discreet photos are snapped. He doesn't even seem to notice. I'm impressed — he's getting better at ignoring the attention. He used to blush so hard his face matched his hair. Now he just makes a beeline for the bar and the empty seat next to me.

"Mate," he greets me, Scots burr firmly in place, "you look like a cup of cold sick."

The bartender, recognizing Sean from our previous visits — and probably the Internet or *Tech Bro Monthly* or something — immediately brings him a double Lagavulin. He whispers something to her and slides his card across the polished granite.

"I saw her tonight."

Sean's brows rise an infinitesimal amount. "Her? The girl from the hotel?"

"Yep." There's no need for anything more. The topic of Aesha is well-trodden ground between us.

"Well, fuck me running." I scrape out a laugh. There's the reason Sean's my best friend. He always knows exactly the right thing to say.

"What are you gonna do about it?"

"There's nothing to do, Sean. She walked away. The end." My gut twists at the memory. There's no way it should still hit me this hard, right? It was a weekend fling. She ran off before the weekend was even over. I have to accept that.

"Uh huh."

"What?"

"I wouldn't be here if you hadn't done something foolish, Teddy Bear."

"Don't pull out my old nickname. You know I hate that."

His laugh is unrepentant. "Then spill your guts, man."

"Fine. I may have asked her to participate in the arts fundraiser I'm leading."

"Because?"

"Because it needs doing, and she's a lawyer. She's probably got connections to a whole bunch of the kind of people we need to support these teachers."

"Convenient access to rich fucks. Noted." I politely neglect to mention that this category includes him, too. "What else?"

"It also means I have a reason to see her again."

"And the reason you want to see her again...?"

"Is because I'm a hopeless idiot. I still want her. Desperately." I finish my scotch and signal for another. The bartender brings over two bowls of chicken curry instead.

"What —"

"You need food, not booze," Sean says. "Eat."

"Thanks, Mom." He gives me the finger. I'm being an ungrateful ass. I deserve it.

"Listen," he says. "Look at this logically —"

"There's nothing logical about this. It's all about my feelings." He makes a face at me, but I go on.

"On the one hand: She is literally amazing. Funny, smart, driven — everything I could want.

"On the other: She walked away and deliberately did not leave me a way to get in touch. That means she was done, right?" Sean shrugs. All this talk about feelings is probably giving him hives.

"But she agreed to work with me on this. Maybe there's still something there? Although it's equally possible that I'm just desperate and will take any scrap of attention she offers."

Sean looks at me for a moment. "Theo. That was the worst case of whiplash I've ever experienced."

"I know. I know. It's crazy. It's making me crazy. I should leave it alone. I should walk away, keep her off the committee, and leave this alone."

"Theo," he says in this gentle, un-Sean like way, and I know where he's going. I want to stop him, but I don't. I came to him because I needed to talk this out with someone who wouldn't pull any punches.

"Is it really her, or is it just that she's the first woman you've felt something for since April died?"

Damn. I saw that coming, and it still hurt like fuck. I take a few bites of my curry to give myself time to think.

"You know April was the absolute love of my life."

"I do." He looks away, trying not to burden me with his own pain. April was his friend, too. "You were broken when you lost her."

"I was. Which is part of the reason this thing with Aesha felt like such a gift. I thought... You only get one person like that in a lifetime, right? The one who supports you, adores you, makes you feel a hundred percent alive? I had that.

"But then I met Aesha, and I felt like... maybe, just maybe, I could have that with her. But she ended it before we could even start."

And that's the crux of the problem, isn't it? I want so much with her, and she's too closed off to go for it.

It's not an unreasonable stance. She's been down this road before, and her divorce has clearly made her gun shy. Not to mention that she has a kid to think about. It makes sense for her to be cautious about bringing someone into his life.

Hell, I might have just pushed too hard. Or I came across as desperate, despite all the work I've done on myself.

"Let me ask you this." Sean keeps his expression neutral. "Do you want this woman so much that you're willing to settle for scraps of her attention?"

I don't answer. I'm honestly not sure. Sean makes a disgusted noise in his throat.

"Theo, you've got the biggest heart of anybody I've ever met. You give to your students, your family, your friends every damned day. If there's a human being on this planet who deserves to be loved with no reservations, I'm pretty sure it's you."

"This is practically a love song from you."

Sean ignores my mockery. "I'm serious. So my advice to you, brother, is don't settle. You're that weird romantic kind of soul who believes in true love. If that's what you want, that's worth holding out for."

My mouth hangs open in shock. Sean and I don't do sincerity. We shoot the shit, we razz each other, we're honest enough to say when the other one's being an ass. A thing we absolutely do not do is offer one another heartfelt compliments. I'm not prepared for the rules to change.

Neither is Sean, it seems. The tips of his ears are purple with embarrassment. He tosses off a casual "Love you, man. I gotta go" before practically running out of the bar.

The bartender tells me to take my time; Sean's already paid. Of course he has. I finish my meal and head home.

I should send her an email. Tell her thanks, but no thanks. There's no need for her to be part of the task force. She shouldn't have to be part of this because I'm desperate.

I'm this close to offering Aesha an out when I check my work email. Among the many messages, I spy one from Pat Saunders.

Congratulations on getting some of our busiest parents to join the committee. Having both Ms. Parker and Ms. Shah is a real coup! I'm certain they will be fantastic contributors to the project. Bravo!

Well, shit. That settles that. Back to the original plan. Surely I can handle this. I'm a professional, for fuck's sake. Just being around Aesha won't turn me into a raving sex maniac who can't control himself. I close the laptop and head downstairs to do a quick evening yoga session.

She had this look on her face tonight, though. That moment when she offered me her personal number as well as her work contacts. For a minute, I saw a flash of... something. Like she meant something more by it. Almost like she wanted to give me — give us — a second chance. What if that's what she was asking, and I cut her off without hearing her out first?

I snort. My unruly imagination is getting away from me. I've put it to good use for the last few months. I damn near ruined my wrists, using my right hand as a miserable substitute for the sweet softness of Aesha wrapped around me.

Sean's words come back to me while I'm holding a pose. He's known me since college, when we were just two scared freshmen trying to figure out how to survive in an environment where we knew no one. The guy is loyalty personified. I'm grateful to have a buddy like that, but it makes him generous when it comes to me. I try to be a decent guy, but I know I'm as much a selfish asshole as anybody else.

Still, he's right about this. Despite losing April, I still want commitment. I still believe in forever — or as long as the universe will let you have. As lovely as she is, and as much as I want her, Aesha isn't on the same page. I need to respect that she doesn't want something real. At least not with me.

I also need to have enough respect for myself not to settle.

Resolved, I shower and head off to bed. I'm determined to ensure this relationship stays strictly professional.

No matter how much it hurts.

Forty-five minutes of chaos.

My first session as a member of Theo's arts fundraising committee — that's what it turns out I agreed to be part of — has been a hot mess.

It's not even that anyone's trying to be difficult. But this combination of PTA regulars and newbies like me who didn't know enough to say no to the hot principal isn't jelling. Herding cats would be easier than this.

"Thank you, everyone," Pat Saunders says. Her smile is polite but strained. "Now I understand some folks want to bring back the old traditions, like the bake sales, and others prefer something newer, like an auction. There is room for compromise here."

Everyone jumps in at once.

"The sheer number of food allergies in our school's third grade class alone —"

"Do we really need an exclusionary event like this proposed auction? What does that say for families in poorer neighborhoods?"

"We should lobby for more state funding to support this arts program —"

"Excuse me, everyone," Though his voice is quiet, Theo commands the group's attention. "I appreciate everyone's contributions to the discussion. Before we narrow down our plans, let's be sure we've heard from everyone who wants to contribute. Are there other suggestions?"

He scans the conference table, making eye contact with everyone. When he reaches me, a brow lifts, like he wants me to speak up. I'm still trying to get a feel for the group; I give him a subtle shake of my head.

I watch him as he continues around the table. I bet he was great in the classroom. The gentle way that he talks to people, making sure they feel heard — that's the magic of who he is. I can't help but admire that.

"We need to make it personal."

"Ms. Shah?"

Damn it. I didn't mean to say that aloud. "Sorry, I didn't intend to share that yet."

"No, please," Theo encourages. "I want to hear your thoughts."

"We've gotten ahead of ourselves," I say. "We need to step back from specific fundraising ideas for a second and take a bird's-eye view. We need to brand this campaign. This has got to be about inspiration."

"How so?" someone asks.

"We're all here because we value education, right? For a lot of us, that value came because we had a teacher who inspired us. Someone who saw and nurtured us, who encouraged our potential. What if we reached out to former students? Get them to talk about the teachers who helped them become who they are now?"

"I like that." This is the first genuine smile I've seen from Pat all night. "Tell me how it helps us raise money."

"It's twofold. We can use our fundraising ideas with these stories. Maybe we don't do a bake sale — but we connect the memory of bake sales to an alum who is now a professional baker.

Or someone who took art, who participated in a student art auction, and then grew up to be a sculptor."

"We're telling origin stories."

"Exactly." The committee members' expressions seem positive. Some of them look at Theo, who is nodding enthusiastically. I keep going.

"You're showing how one little acorn — these classes — grew a massive tree full of talent. Arts funding helped create these adults, these members of the community who bring beauty and art and genius to the world. Once we get that idea into people's heads, then it's a short step to asking for contributions to help the next generation of students become artists and professionals and whatever else they want to be."

Theo's smile takes my breath away with its perfection. I'm absurdly proud that he likes my off-the-cuff idea.

"Thanks for that suggestion, Aesha," he says. "It has real possibilities."

"I agree." Pat sounds relieved. "How about you two flesh out a campaign and present it to the group next time we meet?"

"Great," I lie. "That would be great."

Just before we adjourn, everyone consults their calendars and confirms the date and time for the next meeting. Theo and Pat usher people out, making small talk with them as they go. Normally, I'd be the first one dashing out of the conference room, but now I'm hanging back, watching the crowd dissipate. My whole body is taut with tension.

Theo makes his way over to me. Even in this setting, when I should only be thinking about the job we're here to do and the weight of that responsibility, watching him cross the room makes my mouth go dry.

"Very persuasive, counselor. If that's what you can do on the fly, I'd love to see you in court when you've had a chance to prepare."

"It's pretty impressive," I tease. "I don't know if you're ready for that." Shit. I'm flirting. Why am I flirting?

Heat warms the back of my neck. Ridiculous. I'm a grown woman with a career, not a teenager with a crush. One little compliment from a man shouldn't turn me into a saucy vixen. Even if it's the man I am desperate to get naked with again.

I clear my throat. "We should figure out when we can get together and work on this presentation. I'm not in court for the next two weeks, so that should make it easier."

"What are you doing right now? Do you need to be anywhere?"

"No," I say, ignoring the way my heart starts to pitter patter. "I am free to work my ass off."

"There's a little French place not far from here. It's a quick walk."

"Let's go."

Theo helps me with my coat. The brush of his hand over my shoulders, even through the layers of fabric, feels painfully intimate. He holds the door for me as we leave. The heat of his palm on my lower back as we enter the restaurant makes me swoon a little. Logically, I know this is a working meeting. That doesn't change the fact that it sure seems like a date.

When the waiter brings out a charcuterie board, I glance at Theo's eyes. His expression is guileless. Maybe I'm the only one of us remembering that first night. How he offered to let me just walk away — and the relief in his eyes when I didn't. The way he listened so intensely. How he laughed at my churro addiction like it was the cutest thing in the world. The way he tied me up and made me scream —

"Aesha. Are you all right?" His voice cuts into my reverie. I take a gulp of my wine.

"Yeah," I say. "Fine."

"You seem a little flushed..."

I wave it off. "Just fired up about this fundraiser!" He snorts, knowing I'm full of shit. Still, he goes along with the change of subject. He's probably as eager to be done with this as I am.

It takes us an hour to rough out a strategy for the presentation, complete with a map of the overall plan and my terrible stick figure drawings of what the slides might look like. When we're finished, he leans back in satisfaction. I bite my lip, watching the stretch of his muscles beneath his suit.

"How's Riz doing?" I'm startled by the switch to a personal subject. I didn't expect us to go there.

"He's good. Having a sleepover with the grandparents."

"How are the tuba lessons?"

"Loud." Theo laughs, gives my hand a gentle squeeze. That simple touch scalds me. "Hang in there. It'll be worth it, in the end."

"Promise?" I ask. Theo's eyes meet mine, and for a second, neither of us is thinking about music anymore. He swallows, closes his eyes, and looks away. When he opens them again, I can almost see his entire body retreat from this conversation.

Thankfully, the waiter returns to offer more wine. I take it; I'll get a car back home. Theo declines and requests the check.

Maybe it's the alcohol talking. Maybe it's my hormones. Regardless, this feels like a put-up-or-shut-up moment. I need to be brave. Bold. Decisive.

When our server walks away, I smooth my hair and step into the breach.

"Theo, this is stupid."

"Don't." His voice is jagged, raw. "Please."

"We can't just ignore what happened between us."

"That was for the best. We agreed."

"Did we? You decided. I went along." I reach out and deliberately stroke his hand, echoing his earlier gesture. His quiet, sharp intake of breath lets me know he's as affected as I am.

"Aesha..." My eyes meet his. They're smoldering with banked heat. I refuse to look away.

"I'm being honest." I lick my lips. His gaze flies to my mouth. He makes fists of his hands, like he's fighting the urge to reach for me.

"We had something between us. I think we still do. I am not willing to fight that anymore."

Theo's nostrils flare, and he starts to speak. Abruptly, he thinks better of it, finding our waiter and settling the bill. When he returns, he holds out a hand. I take it.

We walk out of the restaurant. I glance up at him. Energy radiates from him like a physical thing, tying us together. I'm not sure where we're going, but I follow his lead.

In the parking garage, I follow him up two flights of stairs. He lets me in to a dark blue BMW and demands my address. Breathless, I give it to him. I've dreamt of him in my bed for weeks. Now I get to live out that fantasy in the flesh.

We park in my driveway, walking up the slight incline in silence. My hands are so shaky that I can barely undo the lock. Once we're inside, I barely get a second to drop my bag before he's on me. His kiss is ruthless, aggressive, destroying me and putting me back together all at once. I give back as good as I get, tongues and teeth clashing in a battle we are both determined to win.

"Do you have any idea what I want to do to you right now?" he whispers against my mouth. "How the way I need you is like a physical ache in my chest?"

His hands pin mine to the wall.

"It would be so easy, Aesha." His words are jolts of electricity against my skin. "So easy to pull this blazer off — but only halfway, so it ties your hands. I'd strip off this blouse. Taste those gorgeous tits. Get my hands underneath that skirt, inch by careful inch, and slip two fingers inside you?"

I can't stop the moan his words induce. I'm desperate for him to just do it. Already, I'm shivering with need.

"And just when you're on the brink, I'd slip my cock inside you. Get balls deep. Just lose myself in your warm, wet heat."

His breathing is harsh, uneven, like he can't quite get enough air. "Is that what you want, too?"

"You know I do." I shrug my jacket off my shoulders. Theo stops me, pulling away.

"And then what?"

"Then we do it again, if there's time," I laugh, reaching for him. He grabs my hand and holds it to his chest. His heart races beneath our palms.

"That's the problem." His eyes bore into me. "It's not just about sex for me."

Damn it. This was a mistake.

I should have known. I thought — I hoped — we could just enjoy one another. No expectations, no demands. We could just be.

But that's not who Theo is. He's an all in kind of guy. And even though I want him more than my next breath, I refuse to go down this road of commitment again. I won't.

"Okay." Fuck this pressure behind my eyes. I cannot cry. I will not cry.

"I'm not built for casual, Aesha." He stares into my eyes, as if he can make me understand by force of will. "I need more than that."

"I — don't have anymore to give."

Theo hangs his head for a moment. His entire body goes still. When his eyes finally meet mine, the hurt in them snatches my breath away. We stay like that until he laughs, a ragged sound with no humor in it. His palm grazes my cheek. I close my eyes, leaning into the tenderness.

"You're not there." He plants a kiss on my forehead. "It's okay."

That's the first lie he's ever told me.

"When Wendy gets the deck in order, I'll have her send it for your approval." He runs a hand through his hair. "If there are any more changes that need to be made, we should do those over email."

"Okay." The logical part of my brain agrees that staying away from each other makes sense. We want different things. We should leave this alone.

The rest of me, though, hates him a little for making that very logical choice. He's pushing me away — at my request — but somehow I'm the one left with a knot in my gut and tears I refuse to shed.

"I'm gonna go." He gives my hand a last squeeze. "Be well."

I close the door behind him. The finality of it echoes loudly in my head.

This is for the best. Really. I know we had a great time together, but that was a weekend. Not real life, with our jobs and our families and our daily responsibilities. In the real world, Theo and I could never work. No sense putting myself through that again.

I putter around the house, desperately not thinking about the look on Theo's face when I said I had nothing to give. I try to read a book but give up when I realize I've read the same page five times in a row. What the hell is wrong with me? I don't know.

A text from my ex interrupts my maudlin thoughts.

> Riz' shoe size pls?

> Youth 2.

> Thx. Gita recommends these. Saturday ok to drop off?

> Sure.

> K. I want her to meet R. We shd discuss.

> Your sisters like her.

Ha. Should've known they'd tell you.

I'm sure she's lovely. Can't wait to meet her.

I hope you like her too.

And I hope you find your someone soon.

I start to reply with a crossed fingers emoji but can't see enough to send it. What is it with these stupid tears again?

I'm not sad about Vikram. My ex is a good man. We're far better as friends than we were as a couple. He deserves happiness.

And maybe, just maybe, I do, too.

I dig around in my purse. I'm not sure what I'm searching for is still there. When my hand closes on the postcard, I pull it out and stare at it for a long time.

They say that it's insanity to keep doing what you always did and expecting something different. So now it's time for me to actually do something different.

I only hope it's worth it — and that when I'm done, there will still be a chance for Theo and me.

Theo

We did it once, we can do it again. That's what I keep telling myself.

The presentation Aesha and I created for the fundraiser was a success. So much so that the rest of the committee took it up. They helped us refine and polish it, and now we've brought it to the district for their approval. Now we're spending a Friday night outside a conference room, waiting to hear if they'll support our campaign.

Well, I'm sitting. Aesha is pacing, checking emails and leaving voice memos for her assistant. It's like a scene out of a movie, watching her flip from one task to another. Running my school is an enormous responsibility, but her law firm takes up at least as much of Aesha's time. I wonder if she needs more staff.

Not my pig, not my farm, as my students like to say. I have to leave that alone. Despite our last working meeting nearly turning into hallway sex, Aesha and I have stayed one hundred percent professional since. Mostly by avoiding each other.

No working dinners, no visits to either of our homes, and

especially no time alone. Just emails and committee meetings in which we address each other formally as Ms. Shah and Mr. Kearney. No hints at all that we ever meant anything to each other. That we might have had a future together.

Although we've been so very careful to avoid anything personal, I've noticed there's something different about her lately. She seems... lighter, somehow. It confirms that closing the door on our relationship was the right thing to do. That freed her up to think less about us and move on. If it's like torture for me? That's my burden to live with.

The conference room door opens. One of the board members ushers us both inside.

"Congratulations, Mr. Kearney," the chairwoman announces. "We love this plan. The board is excited to help fund your committee's proposal."

"Thank you," I say. "But the idea was all Ms. Shah's."

"Which couldn't have happened without Mr. Kearney and the rest of the committee," Aesha interjects. "We appreciate your confidence in us."

There's more chitchat, a few details to work out, but we confirm that we'll handle those in subsequent meetings. Aesha and I manage to exit the conference room, and the building, without embarrassing ourselves. As soon as we get to the parking lot, she turns to me.

"Holy shit, Theo." Her smile is radiant. "We did it!"

"We really did." I offer her a hand. "Bravo!"

She ignores my hand, throwing her arms around me. For a second, I'm too surprised to move. Then I relax into it. This is okay. Just a friendly hug between colleagues. We can do friendly. I do not smell her hair, with that subtle mix of coconut and citrus. Nor do I revel in the feel of her soft, soft curves pressed against me. Nope. Absolutely not.

"We should celebrate. Do you want to get a drink?" Aesha's face is open, hopeful. Glowing with our success. If it were anyone else, I would happily celebrate this moment with them. But this truce, or whatever we want to call it, feels too fragile to risk.

"That's —" I clear my throat. "I don't think that's a good idea."

"Oh. I — I didn't mean —" she stammers. The flush in her cheeks and her sudden breathlessness confirm that she's remembering that moment in her hallway as much as I am. Hurt flashes across her face so quickly I almost miss it. Fuck. I hate this.

"It's not that I don't — we should —"

"Of course." She holds up a hand to stop my babbling. Nothing I could possibly say would make this hurt less.

"You'll email the other members of the committee? Let them know how we did?"

"Absolutely." She sticks out a hand. The formality of it, after what we've been to each other, after everything... I hold back a sour laugh. It is what it is. No sense infecting her with my bitter disappointment.

Her skin is cool and smooth next to mine. I almost forget to let go.

"See you at the next committee meeting?" I ask. She nods. We say goodbye, go our separate ways to our cars, to a long, lonely night of nothing and no one special.

I'm too restless to go straight home. I need a drink. Somewhere in public, so I won't be tempted to leave a very personal, overly vulnerable message on her work voicemail.

Before I know it, I'm in the parking lot of Hotel d'Amour. I don't examine why I came here. Hell, maybe returning to the scene of the crime will help. I get a room, then head straight for the bar. I need to get something strong in my system to wipe her off my mind.

Two glasses of Macallan 12 later, I've realized my plan won't work.

Being here makes the memories of us more potent. All I can see is the face she makes when telling a dirty joke — saucy, but also a tiny bit embarrassed. I see the curve of her hip under my hand, the lush brown of her nipples beneath my tongue. The tenderness of her mouth under mine.

I stare into my current glass of whisky. Damn. This must be stronger than I thought. I can smell her perfume. It's distinct and complicated, something like roses and oranges and a bunch of things that make me want to devour her.

"Theo." I turn with a jolt, and she's there, in the flesh. Fuck me. How is it that no matter how perfect my memory of her is, the reality is always so, so much more? I'm doomed.

"What are you doing here?" My tone is harsher than I intend. She winces a little at my coldness.

"I still wanted to celebrate our accomplishment, even if we couldn't do it together. And I needed a little time to myself."

Me too. Me fucking too. And yet, here she is, close enough to touch. Wrecking me with nothing more than a glance from those gorgeous eyes.

"I can go," she offers. I shake my head. This isn't that big a town. We're going to run into each other often enough. I should get used to it. Still, I brace myself when she takes the seat next to me. For what, I don't know.

The bartender offers me a refill. I direct it Aesha's way instead. She thanks me, but there's no need. It's an excuse to look in the gilded mirror above the bar and watch the long line of her throat as she swallows it down. Our eyes meet in the mirror. Hers go wide at whatever she sees in mine.

I look away. My desire is too bold, too obvious. It's making her uncomfortable. Fuck this. I throw back the rest of my drink and stand up. She can have the bar. I'll have a pity party in my room.

She lets out a big breath. Lays a hand on my arm.

"Theo," she says again. It sounds like it hurts. Like it matters to her. Like I matter to her.

"Now that we've got city approval, you don't have to stay on the task force, Aesha." The skin of my arm heats beneath her touch, despite the layers of fabric between her skin and mine. I focus my attention there. It stops me thinking about how badly I want to kiss her.

"No?" She smiles, but it doesn't reach her eyes. "Am I getting kicked out for bad behavior?"

"It's not you, it's me." The cliché slips out before I even realize it. We look at each other and then burst into laughter.

"I mean it," I tell her after our laughter subsides. "I'm ninety percent certain you only agreed to help in order to make me stop talking. Your input has been excellent, but I don't want to force you into working with me."

"I only agreed to it because it meant I got to see you," she counters. "I didn't even know what the task force was supposed to do."

"Aesha —"

"No, please. Let me finish. I have just enough courage left to say this."

It's the *please* that gets me. I sit back down.

"I'm a little bit of a mess, you know." Her expression turns rueful. "Not with work, or with my family — I've got those under control. I pride myself on that. I never miss a deadline, and I'm always there when my son needs me. Emotionally, though — I've kept people at arm's length for a really long time. I didn't want to fail again.

"Our weekend made me feel... reckless. Daring. Bold. Sexy. I loved it.

"But it also overwhelmed me. You, with your warmth and your tenderness, you just blew past all my barriers, and I didn't know how to stop it. I wasn't even sure I wanted to stop it. I was barreling headlong into something I couldn't control. It scared the shit out of me."

"So you left."

"So I left," she repeats. "I've regretted it ever since."

I'm stunned.

"Say something," she demands. "I have to report back to my therapist."

This woman. She's so brave. And she always seems to be a step ahead of me. I have to try to match her again.

"When I lost my wife," I say, "I was sure I was permanently broken. I dated occasionally, after a year or two. But my heart? Closed door. I threw myself into my work so I could avoid even having to try anything that looked like a relationship.

"But then I met you, Aesha. You blew those doors wide open. I fell hard and fast, and all I've been able to think about since then is how much I want to be with you for as long as you'll let me."

Her grip on my arm tightens. I cover her hand with my own.

"Still? You want to be with me?" She says the words like she can't quite believe them, like her luck is too much to believe in. "Even though I was so afraid of this?"

"I always want to be with you," I say. "I don't care if you were afraid. Just stay with me now. We'll get braver together."

I'm not sure which of us reaches out first; it doesn't matter. But when our lips meet, it's like the answer to a prayer. Her mouth is decadent, and every single second I'm near it is heaven. We kiss until we can't breathe and have to come up for air, chests heaving and hands shaking with need.

The elevator ride is a blur. Our hands and bodies demand that we touch from the second we leave the bar until we make it inside the room. Then it's a fight to stay apart long enough to get out of our clothes. We finally manage to get naked and start to re-learn the language of one another. This time, she takes control and blindfolds me with my own tie. She's eager to discover which strokes make me shudder, and her hands and mouth write a poem of pleasure all over my body. But when she takes me in her mouth, I give up the blindfold. The sight of her full, glossy red lips wrapped around my cock is too good to miss.

I warn her that I'm close, but when her response is to grab my ass and dig in, I can't hold back any longer. The orgasm races through me like a rocket, originating in my balls and ending somewhere around the stratosphere.

When I come back down to earth, she's lazily stroking my chest, preening like a cat.

"So I take it you liked that," she says.

"Absolutely not," I say, wiggling my eyebrows at her like a crazed Muppet. She does this cute laugh that I instantly want to hear again. "I loved it."

"Well, if you're a very good boy," she says huskily, "there's more where that came from."

I intend to hold her to that promise. I can't wait.

Aesha

I'm blindfolded yet again.

Even though the circumstances are different from the usual, I have to laugh. I don't understand why this is the theme of my relationship, but I'll take it.

My love and my son help me out of the car and onto the sidewalk, steadying me when I stumble. Smoothly, as if they planned it, Theo grips my left hand while Riz holds my right. I'm so lucky with the two of them. When Theo and I decided to give this a real try, we kept it cool in front of Riz. We wanted to protect him if it — if we — didn't work out.

Of course, I forgot to account for my kid being a little smarty pants. Riz figured out pretty quickly that most of my "meetings" with Mr. Kearney had nothing to do with fundraising. When I confessed that we were dating, I got an epic tween eye roll and a "Duh. Mr. K's cool, Mom. Whatever."

They've bonded over tuba lessons and baseball and a truly shocking number of hair products. I only understand about half of what they're talking about at any given moment, but their affection for each other is one of my biggest joys.

And it's not just my son. My extended family, my parents, and my sister have all embraced him wholeheartedly. They are grateful that he makes me slow down. That Theo insists on me taking time for myself instead of working so hard I only eat cheese doodles for dinner.

Tonight, for example, rather than our usual Friday night pizza, Theo suggested we get dressed up and go out. He claimed that we should celebrate the success of our fundraising campaign, which raised funds for five new art and music teachers. I'm pretty proud of my role in that, so I agreed.

But Riz, who has never met a T-shirt he didn't like, is wearing a tie without a complaint. And when I asked my sister about her plans for tonight, she hemmed and hawed in an extremely suspicious way. Then Theo suggested the blindfold, confirming that something was up.

They're so busted.

I didn't plan to make a big deal about my birthday, but if they want to 'surprise' me with a nice evening out, I'm happy to let them.

A door creaks, and my guys walk me inside. The buzz of murmuring voices, and the clink of plates and glassware are enough to clue me in. We're back at our favorite steak place. I can almost smell the ribeye already.

The noise of the main dining room dims as another door closes behind me.

Riz undoes the blindfold. When my eyes focus again, I spot my parents and sister, looking excessively pleased with themselves, my aunts and uncles, and five of my cousins. I tear up. I love that Theo and my family have gone to all this trouble for me.

Then I spy Theo's friend Sean, smug expression firmly in place, as well as Theo's older sisters and his parents. We've all gotten to know each other over the past year, and wonder of wonders, they've started to feel like my family almost as much as his. We visited them in California just last month. I'm so grateful that they made the trip.

Oddly, the one person I don't see is Theo himself. Where did he get to?

"Turn around, Mom," Riz tells me.

When I do, I see the love of my life, down on one knee in front of me, holding out a deep blue velvet box. My heart starts to race.

"Aesha," he says, voice full of emotion, "I had an entire speech planned. It was really beautiful, too. But Riz reminded me that simple is best — and also that you hate to be kept waiting when steak is involved."

I fake glare at my family and friends for laughing at that.

"Instead, what I have to say is this: Thank you for the most incredible year. Even though I'm the teacher, I've learned so much from you about how to be a good partner, a good parent, and a good man.

"I know it's your birthday, but would you please give me the gift of having the most wonderful woman in the world become my wife?"

I fan myself frantically, trying to hold back the tide of my tears.

But it's impossible. Just like saying anything but yes would be impossible. This man is my everything. He's not perfect, but he's perfect for me.

I pull him up from the ground and kiss him senseless. I don't have the words, but I want him to feel exactly how much I love him.

A dramatic throat clearing beside me brings another round of laughter from our friends and family. I look down at my son, planting a smooch on his forehead.

"I assume that's a yes?" Theo whispers. He slides the ring on my finger. The weight of it is like my feelings for him: solemn and joyful all at once.

"Maybe. If you promise to let me spend the rest of my life proving what a brilliant choice you made."

"YOLO, right?" He gives me a smart-aleck grin.

"Absolutely."

Belong to Me

Mala

I have got to get out of here.

Don't get me wrong. It's wonderful to see my big sister happy. And Aesha is surely happier than I've ever seen her. We're at her favorite restaurant, at a party she thought was for her birthday. Instead, her boyfriend Theo popped the question. She said yes, of course, and now she's gliding around the room, hand in hand with her brand new fiancé.

Holy shit, my sister has a fiancé. How the hell did that happen? She swore she'd never get married again. But here she is, glowing like a fucking flashlight, showing off the ring to all of the cousins and parents and aunties and uncles, making it clear to the whole world that she's entirely, insanely in love with this man.

And Theo's no better. He's gaga over her. The man would literally drink her bath water if she asked him to do it.

They're so gross, the both of them. Totally in love with one another. All this lovey-dovey sweetness is giving me a headache.

To be fair, that might also be the three — no, four — no — the *several* cocktails I've had since this party began. Delicious, but I will be feeling those tomorrow. Right now, it's time for me to pull an Irish exit, as my friend Siobhan says. The aunties are one drink away from looking at my unmarried ass and asking questions I have no desire to answer. I grab my wrap and head for the door.

My nephew Riz catches me just before I get there.

"Sneaking off again, Auntie Em?" He is the model of tween ennui, tossing his floppy hair to the side, with his arms folded across his teeny little preteen chest. He gives me a side eye that would daunt a lesser woman.

"Watch it, bub. I'm more like the Wicked Witch." I kiss my gorgeous boy on the cheek. "Cover for me with Nana and Nani, eh?"

"It'll cost you." The saucy twinkle in his eye reminds me so much of my sister. She was feisty even when we were young.

"What is this, extortion?" I ask in mock indignation. "And your mother's a lawyer. Are you really going to shame her with this life of crime you're leading?"

"Nana and Nani are *your* parents, but you're dodging them," he points out. Kid's got me there.

"Such disrespect, beta! How dare?"

Smart boy that he is, he doesn't take the bait. He merely gives me a raised eyebrow, and holds out his hand. I crack up.

"Fine, fine," I say, handing over the gift I had meant to give him anyway. "Here's your stinking game card. I guess I don't know anyone else with an Xbox."

He thanks me profusely, and I even get a hug. That's practically an "I love you" coming from a kid who is entirely too cool for school. My cold, dead heart is slightly warmed.

I slip through the door of the private dining room and shut it gently behind me. Whew. I take a deep breath and lean back against the old-growth fir door, enjoying the quiet. I adore my family. They're loud, opinionated and unapologetic about any of it. But all that love and togetherness is making me tense. I need to find a quick release for all that pressure. When I get back to my condo, I am so pulling out the 'friends with bennies' roster to see who's up next.

"Mala."

Shit. That gravelly voice and ridiculous Scottish burr can only be one person. I thought I'd gotten away clean.

"Fuck me," I mutter.

"Any place you want, any time you like, gorgeous."

That shouldn't make my nipples tighten or my nether regions throb. But between the accent and the alcohol, I'm a hot, horny mess. Scowling, I turn around to face my nemesis.

"That would be the 31st of never, thanks," I lie, as I walk away.

"Wait."

"What do you want, Sean?"

That's, right. Sean. As in Sean Fucking Reid: tech bro, sometime philanthropist, and asshole gazillionaire. Just standing there, with his six feet tallness and his green eyed-ness and his absurdly taut abs. The so-called Ginger Genius of the Pacific Northwest.

"You know what I want, lass." His eyes rake over me. I growl at him in response. Shockingly, the force of my scorn does not instantaneously make him wither and die.

"You're right, I do. Remind me why I should care?"

"Because Theo is my best friend in the entire world, and he's marrying your sister."

"He's your only friend," I point out. "Which makes him a freaking saint."

"Which means," he corrects, "that you and I will be spending a lot of time together, as maid of honor and best man."

What the fu — did I agree to that? Sounds like bullshit. Why would I agree to anything that meant I had to spend more time with this ... this... pfft. My brain can't even come up with an adjective scathing enough for my least favorite human.

But then the memory hits me. Somewhere around the third — or was it fourth?— toast to the happy couple. Our Uncle Yasir had started to tell the story about Aesha and me accidentally setting their shed on fire, and Auntie Priyanka made him stop, since it was thirty years ago and obviously we had turned out fine, and the shed was ugly anyway and there was no reason to bring it up at this blessed occasion, etc., etc.

Somewhere in there, Aesha threw her arm around me.

"I love him so much, Mala. Like so, so, so much."

I snort laughed. My straitlaced lawyer sister gushing like that? She had to be blitzed.

"I never thought I'd want to get married again, but he's just... so wonderful. And hot. Like soooooooooo crazy hot. There was this one time —"

I held up a hand. "Whoa. Settle down there, sister. I have to see this man over the dinner table at Thanksgiving for the rest of my life. Please do not overshare."

"Good point." She hiccuped quietly into her palm. "But it's all because of you. This relationship happened because of you. You're the best."

I had given her a smug smile. "Maybe now you'll take my advice about those dreadful slippers, too. Since this worked out so well."

"Give up my Crocs? Never." She stuck out her tongue at me. "The only shoes you have a say in are the ones you wear as my maid of honor."

"Aww. You like me. You really like me."

"Hush, you. Who else would I want? Besides, you and Sean will look so great together in the photos. I can't wait."

Ugh. I rub my temple at the memory. Fine. I agreed to this. That doesn't mean I have to like it.

"It's not like this is their first rodeo, Sean," I say now. "There won't be too many 'duties' for us to handle."

He quirks one ginger eyebrow at me, oddly reminding me of Riz just moments ago.

"Are you kidding? Theo's found the love of his life, for the second time. That lucky bastard is getting every party I can possibly throw him."

I blink in shock at this declaration. *The* Sean Reid turns out to be a sentimental fool. I'm sure that information didn't make the cover of *Wired* magazine. His rep would be ruined.

"Besides," he continues, "I overheard your aunties in there. They are not going to let this marriage be some kind of fly-by-night operation."

Damn it. I hate that he's right. My family would disown Aesha and me before they'd allow anything less than a full-scale Bollywood production for this wedding.

"Maybe so. Still, until concrete plans are in place, we literally have no reason to speak to one another." I declare. "So whatever you were gonna say can wait."

"All I want is to make sure this all goes smoothly. That means you and I need to bury the hatchet."

I know exactly where I'd like to bury it. Right in the middle of his stupid perfect pecs. From the look on his face, Sean knows it too.

He holds up his hands in mock surrender.

"I get it. You hate me now. I accept that." Something like regret washes over his face. "But don't Theo and Aesha deserve to have the perfect celebration? Can we put aside our differences long enough to do this for them?"

"Fine." The word comes out in that same clipped way my mom says it when she's annoyed with us. "As long as you understand this is strictly for their benefit. We are not friends. I do not like you. And after this is over, I plan to forget that you exist."

"Yes, Mala."

"And don't assume I'm going to change my mind."

"Wouldn't dream of assuming anything at all when it comes to you." His eyes darken as he looks me over again. A flare of heat blooms inside me in response.

What the hell? As long as I have to spend time with him, I might as well get something out of it.

"One more thing."

"Yes?"

I come closer, pressing my body against his. Sean sucks in a breath at my sudden closeness. He lets me walk him backward until he's pinned against the wall. He wraps an arm around my waist, tips my chin up with the other hand. When I lick my lips, his eyes rake across my mouth, greedily searching for an excuse to do more than just look. Slowly, torturously, I put my hands on his chest, lightly raking my nails over his nipples. He hisses out a curse.

"Mala..." he whispers. There's an unspoken question in those green eyes that I'm all too eager to answer.

"Meet me at my place in thirty minutes," I whisper. "Bring condoms. Lots of them."

Sean

EIGHTEEN MONTHS AGO

"There has to be a bar in this bloody hotel, doesn't there?" After nine torturous hours of meetings, I am desperate for a drink.

"Mister Reid," Cameron begins. Uh oh. My assistant is using my surname. He may as well have added *you bloody idiot*. I hear it in his voice.

"Your lawyers have called. Multiple times. We really need to schedule a meeting —"

"Cam, I'm begging you," I say. "I need a wee break. Five minutes at least. I'm not firing on all cylinders at the moment."

His eager expression turns into a frown.

"That depends. How much do we want to fail?"

"You're sassy this evening."

"I'm right, Sean. You want to start a foundation. This is what building it up looks like."

I groan. I know Cameron is right, sassy response notwithstanding. When I took my company public, it was strategic. The IPO raised billions of dollars and made me filthy rich. But

I don't want to be an arsehole with too much money and not enough ambition — I intend to make real, lasting change in this world.

So I hired an assistant with a fancy degree in nonprofit management (and seemingly endless reserves of patience) to help me figure out how to do it. But I never dreamed trying to do some good would involve so much glad-handing, or so many people trying to kiss my arse and make me like it. This process sucks.

All I want is a glass of Bunnahabhain 18 and a few minutes of silence. I convince Cameron that a thirty minute break won't hurt our progress and we head to the hotel's bar. I can practically taste the scotch already.

But when I get there, instead of polite renditions of jazz standards and soft-spoken bartenders, there's a symphony of cables, lights and an enormous movie camera.

"Mr. Reid, I'm so sorry," the bartender says. I try not to frown at her. It's not her fault that I'm still not used to everyone knowing my name. I've been Internet famous for a decade, but that's an order of magnitude less terrible. Apparently being a billionaire makes you famous like a Hemsworth.

"The bar is closed for the evening due to some promotional work," she tells me. "I'm happy to get a table for you and your guest at our restaurant instead. Or if you'd prefer, I can send a staff member with a mobile bar up to your suite."

I hope my face doesn't show my horror. The poor girl's just trying to do her job. She couldn't know I'd sooner eat glass than have another person in my space right now. I'd hoped to sit here quietly, away from people. This mobile bartender sounds like torture.

I decline her offer and contemplate my options. There's already a decent drinks cart in the penthouse suite, although it doesn't have my preferred Scotch. I could send Cameron off to the bottle shop, but if there's one thing that screams rich prick, asking your highly trained and very professional assistant to fetch you a particular kind of alcohol to soothe your feelings is probably it.

"Young Cameron," I say. "It's after six. Why don't you go home for the night?" He starts to protest, but I keep going. "Make the appointment with the lawyers in the morning. I promise, I will be sure to attend the meeting. But we're done right now. Go home to your...cat or whatever."

He scoffs. "You don't know that I have a cat."

I give him the old side eye. He's the most tightly wound person I know. Invasions have been planned less closely than the schedules he creates for me. The kid is definitely a Cat Person.

"Fine," he sniffs. "I have a cat. But Freya's being fed by my partner. I can stay."

I'm about to reply when the call goes out: "Quiet on the set." It's too late for us to walk out without interrupting, so Cameron and I park ourselves in a corner.

"And...action!" the director calls out, but I'm not sure where to look. Then I hear a rich, lush voice.

"Hey everybody, I'm Mala Shah. Welcome to FortyFab, where we show you how to live your hashtag-best-life anywhere in the world."

When I spot her, I see that she's facing away from me. A river of dark, wavy hair flows down her back, with bold red highlights streaking through it. The hair is almost as long as her dress. It's some sort of strapless pleated concoction in cream colored silk. The garment hugs her curves and is just long enough to avoid scandal. Her legs are ridiculously long, and the red-bottomed shoes she wears make them look even longer.

"Today I'm thrilled to introduce you to a place near my hometown," she says. Her voice is beautiful. Almost smoky in its depth. "Welcome to Hotel D."

She starts talking a bit about the history of the place, but I'm not hearing a word she says. I'm too curious about what she looks like to focus on her words. I've been on enough sets to recognize that Cameron and I are trapped in this back corner of the bar for the next few minutes, unless I want to fuck up their shots. Since I'm not about to throw my weight around and demand special treatment, I figure getting to stare at this long-legged goddess is my reward.

My phone vibrates. I pull it out and see a text from Cameron. I glance over at him, frowning in confusion.

> Put your tongue back in your mouth. You look desperate.

There's a winking emoji alongside. I scoff silently.

> You're fired.

> You wouldn't dare.

> Cheeky, yet accurate.

I put the phone away and turn back towards this velvet-voiced siren.

Not to brag, but I've dated my fair share of people whose job it is to be professionally attractive. Yet this odd pull towards Mala Shah is a first. I am desperate to catch a glimpse of her face, but I'm already half in lust with her from the rear view alone.

When she finishes her monologue and turns around, it hits me like a punch to the solar plexus. She's gorgeous. Glowing brown skin, enormous doe eyes, a full mouth that practically begs to be kissed. She is every fantasy I've ever had come to life.

"Who is she?" I mutter to myself.

"She's an Instagram influencer for ladies of a certain age," Cameron pipes up, looking at me like I have two heads. "She does a great travel show, among other things. You've never heard of Forty+Fabulous?"

"I build things on the internet, Cam. I don't use it."

"Someone needs to get out more," he mumbles, just loud enough for me to hear.

I scowl at his unrepentant grin as I watch this stunning woman work.

And it is work. She and the camerawoman consult on other shots of the space. I envy her easy way of working with her crew, the way she charms the very same bartender who told me the space was closed into pulling out a bottle of something dark and expensive and offers a round of shots to her team.

She makes her way over to Cameron and me, those long, long legs gleaming in the light. I immediately imagine how they'd look wrapped around my waist.

Fuck me. I'm halfway to publicly embarrassing myself.

"Hi," she says, offering a handshake. "I'm Mala. I don't think we've met. Are the two of you with the hotel?"

Cameron snorts as I blink in confusion.

She doesn't know who I am. That's ... new.

It's been literal years since I've met someone who didn't already have a freaking dossier on me.

"No," Cameron says, as if he can't quite hold back a laugh, "just a thirsty fan. I am, anyway. Cameron Brown." He shakes her hand and she smiles at him, the charming bastard.

"Glad to hear it, Cameron. And your frowning friend?"

It took me a second to realize that she was referring to myself.

"Sean Reid. And I don't frown."

"No?" The teasing tone in her voice gets under my skin in a way I'm not prepared to contemplate with my assistant right next to me.

"No," I say shortly.

"Hmm. Maybe you're right." She tips her head to the side. I clench my hands into fists when she bites her lip. "It's more of a glower, really."

"I — I don't — glower, either," I sputter. Cameron nearly

chokes with the effort of not laughing. The look I know I'm giving him isn't helping my case.

"Oh, no, you should play that up," she tells me. "It's very hot."

I haven't even known this woman for two minutes, and she's taking the piss. That's got to be a record.

I am slightly alarmed to realize I like it.

"You've got this tall, broad, brooding thing happening— it's very sexy. And the accent too? Whew. Wildly hot."

I don't know what to respond to first: her ruthless assessment of me or the fact that she called me sexy. People are generally too busy trying to suck up to me to tease or to throw compliments my way. But she just came out with it. Wait — does that mean she personally finds me sexy, or was that meant in a more general sense?

While I'm parsing this out, she turns to Cameron. "Would you like to join us for dinner? It'll be a while — maybe 30 minutes or so? The crew's finishing the last of the b-roll, and then they need to pack up the equipment, but we always love to meet fans of the channel."

"I'd be delighted," Cameron beams. That's not an exaggeration. She's got him wrapped around her finger and he's happy to be there. "Let me just call my partner..."

"Bring them too, if you like. The hotel is preparing a spread for us, so we can get the full experience. Like I said, it'll take a bit, so that gives your partner time to get here. It would be great to have you two join us."

I'm a third wheel, watching the two of them gab while I stand there like a complete idiot. There's nothing wrong with me. I can be charming. And she said herself I'm sexy. I can do this.

"Do you want to come up to my suite?" I blurt out. Mala and Cameron both turn to me with wide open eyes and startled expressions. I hasten to explain.

"I — I'm in the penthouse," I clarify. "If you really want to show your fans what the hotel is like, then they should see the nicest room in the place. It'd let you give your audience that full experience you were just talking about."

She eyeballs me for a moment, as if trying to read my mind. I can barely believe I made the offer myself. But there's something about this woman. I feel an almost primal need to be close to her, to spend more time with her anyway I can. If it means offering up a glimpse of my over the top hotel room, so be it.

"That's very kind of you. Mind if I check it out first, before we bring up the whole crew?"

"Right now?"

"Of course. Unless you need a few minutes to get your boxers off of the floor?"

"I'm sure housekeeping's been through to hide any of my indiscretions," I reply. A smile crept onto my face in spite of my determination not to crack. Her matching one is dazzling.

"Then, lead on, Macduff." She puts her arm in mine. "Let me see what you've got."

Mala

EIGHTEEN MONTHS AGO

The scowling Scotsman, it turns out, has a gorgeous smile.

Of course, the rest of him is pretty fantastic, too. Green eyes, ginger hair with a streak of grey in the front, and a bulky build that's just the right amount of muscle.

But that smile. Damn. That's a panty dropper if ever there were one.

I want to give him reasons to smile. Filthy, dirty reasons. Get on my knees kind of reasons.

I'd noticed him right away, lurking in the corner of the bar while I did my spiel on camera. Only my professionalism kept me from stopping the shoot and making a beeline for the enormous dude who stared at me with such intensity. But we filmed for so long today, I didn't dare. Last thing I wanted was to drag out the crew's working hours just so I could ogle the hottie hiding in the shadows.

It's been forever since I was attracted to someone this much or this fast. I can't even remember the last time I saw a guy and I just — *wanted* him. Is it two years? Five? Ever? It's almost a relief to know that side of me isn't broken. I seriously wondered if I'd ever feel that spark again.

But here I am, sparking like mad, with a stunning giant of a man who offered to show me his fancy hotel suite. And I said yes.

I suppress a giggle. This is such a basic porno plot.

He doesn't seem to have pornographic intentions, though. Which is a shame. I very much want to experience those intentions. Downstairs, when he thought I wasn't looking, Sean gave me a look so hot I felt like he'd stripped me bare. But he hasn't said two words to me since we got in this elevator.

"Here we are, then," he says, in that gravelly burr, and leads me out of the elevator. I teased him about that voice just to get a reaction, but it is the absolute truth. Between the accent and the straight out of the movies looks, I bet that hundreds of women fall at his feet all the time. The dude's probably slept his way down the whole West Coast, leaving a trail of well-satisfied ladies in his wake.

That thought is way more arousing than it should be. I decide to interrogate it later.

We walk down the hall toward his suite, our footsteps cushioned by plush, discreet carpet. The decor is muted, tone on tone wallpaper in warm shades of cream, rust and ochre. Strikingly modern brass fixtures light our way. We stop in front of a heavy door with complex carvings and old-fashioned brass hinges and handles. It's stained a deep shade of walnut, but I'm positive it's Douglas fir.

"It's the only suite on this floor," he says. So, you know, privacy."

"That must come in handy," I say. He makes a surprised sort of grunt, somewhere between *I can't believe you said that* and *I am absolutely not dignifying that with an answer.*

Sean enters a code on the very modern lock. He steps back to let me pass.

The suite has the same luxurious feel as the hall. Its creamy walls are like the inside of a ring box, letting the jewel-toned overstuffed furniture — and the baby grand piano — take center stage. A pair of forest green sofas are absolutely covered with contrasting velvet pillows that offer sharp pops of color. They sit in front of a stunning two-sided fireplace. Just beyond it, I catch a glimpse of the dining area and kitchen.

"This is lovely," I say.

"It's bigger than my first flat," he replies, half a smile ghosting across his lips. Even half is compelling; I can't help but return it.

He sounds much more confident than when I teased him downstairs. I'd thrown him off his game, with my little jokes. I got the distinct impression that he liked it.

"Mine, too. First, second, — heck, it might be bigger than the one I live in now."

"You live in town?" he asks, perching on the edge of one sofa. His lingering look at my legs as I sit on the other one gives me a little thrill.

"How's that?"

"You said this place is near your hometown. You're from Oregon, then?"

Interesting. He was actually listening when we recorded. My estimation of him goes up a notch.

"The western suburbs, yeah. There's a pretty big desi community out there."

"Right, I've noticed. Our offices are out there, near the sneaker factory." I snort. That so-called 'factory' is a multibillion dollar company. I appreciate that he's unimpressed.

"What about you? Where are you from?"

"Here and there. Mostly Glasgow. My family's still there." He takes off his tie and rolls up the sleeves of his button down. We've just met, but the action feels intimate, watching him disrobe this little bit. The contrast of slightly tan skin and crisp white cotton is oddly arousing.

"Come on," he says, tucking his tie into a pocket. There's an intensity in his eyes that lures me in. "Let me give you the nickel tour."

Sean takes me from room to room, pointing out the marble-clad bath, with its fancy rain shower head; the live edge dining table paired with antique chairs; the bedrooms on the first level, with gorgeous views of the city's skyline and the way the river threads through the buildings.

"This is perfect for our channel. People will love it."

He grunts in response. I turn to him. He's standing just a little too close. Heat flares in his sea green eyes.

"You disagree?"

"I'm not your audience. It's all a bit much for me," he replies. This man's talent for understatement is impressive.

"Why is that?"

Sean shrugs. "I know I'm staying here and all, but fancy's really not my style. When you live like a toff, people assume who you are, what you're like. Makes them act a bit weird around you."

"Hmm. That sounds like it could get lonely."

He shrugs and gives yet another grunt. This one is something like *Meh. Let's not throw a poor little rich boy pity party.* But the way the tips of his ears go a little pink makes me think I'm on to something.

"Do you want to see the upstairs?" His voice has an edge to it that he can't quite tamp down. Like he's trying so hard to be a gentleman, but he can't quite manage it. I wonder if telling him not to bother would make me a bad person.

"Said the spider to the fly?" I tease.

"Spider? Oh, no. Wrong part of the animal kingdom entirely."

Oh. *There's* that look again. That look, and that smile — the one that is positively filthy with intent — that's what brought me up here.

He comes closer, whispers in my ear. "More like the big bad wolf."

"Too bad I left my red cape at home." I tell him with a wink.

The once-over I get from him in response makes me flush with heat.

He gestures toward the stairs. "After you."

I put a little extra twist in my hips as I head up to the second level. This dress and these heels make my legs look amazing, and I want him to get the full effect. When I reach the top and look back, his slightly dazed expression proves I've succeeded.

Sean opens the door. A massive four-postered California king is the star of the show, carved rails swathed in burgundy velvet curtains. The other furnishings — a chest of drawers, a vanity and chair, a chaise longue on either side of a cocktail table — are simple, the better to show off the masterpiece.

But the view is even more impressive than the bed. I make a beeline toward the enormous windows, the better to drink it in.

The city is laid out before us like a feast. Sumptuous and rich, the glow of the lights bounces off of the river and reflects back onto the ribbons of highway.

"Magnificent," I say to myself. Realizing that I'm still holding my bag, I drop my clutch on the table. I want my hands free for whatever comes next.

"Agreed." I turn back to him, casually leaning in the doorway. I'm instantly ensnared by those eyes. They're bright, like sea glass, and solely focused on me.

"Sean." My tone is gently chiding. His eyes actually have the nerve to twinkle.

"It's not a line, lass," he says. Even though I should know better, that *lass* warms me right down to my toes. "You look damned good framed in that window there. Your camera person should see it."

Right. My camera operator and crew. Who are probably downstairs wondering what the heck is taking me so long. I'm surprised Vonnie isn't blowing up my phone. I dig in my pockets for my cell and pull up the messages.

Oh. Would've helped if I hadn't put the thing on silent. I'm reading through her sixteen texts when Sean comes over to me.

"All right?"

"Yeah." I respond with a thumbs up emoji and put the device away. "Turns out the food arrived just after you and I left. They demolished it and your assistant is now leading them on a bar crawl between here and Vancouver."

"Cameron's a good lad. He won't steer them wrong. Might make for a late start tomorrow, though."

I make an affirmative noise. I'm unnerved by the sudden awareness that my evening is wide open.

"So," I say briskly. "Thank you. For the tour. You're right: filming here would be perfect."

"It was my pleasure," he says. He licks his lip; I am instantly jealous of his tongue.

"If you'll give me Cameron's information, I'll have my assistant reach out to him tomorrow to make arrangements."

"Or...?" He gets even closer to me.

"Or what?" I ask, dazzled by his nearness. He smells delicious. Like pine trees and bad decisions.

"We could do all of that after you let me take you to dinner."

"What if I just want you to take me?"

Sean freezes for a moment, green eyes darkening into molten pools of heat. I hold my breath. Then he explodes into motion, a hand on either side of my face, pulling me toward him. I have just a second to notice the firm press of his body against mine, the solidity of him, all muscle and hardness meeting my soft curves.

Then his mouth is on mine, and his kiss is everything I've ever needed.

Slowly, thoroughly, he dives into me, teasing my tongue with his own. We kiss until we're forced to break apart, just to get some air.

"Oh," I say, breathless. Our foreheads touch. "You are good at this."

He gives me that dirty, dirty smile again. "You've no idea. Turn around."

When I do as he asks, I realize the window acts like a mirror. I watch him slide the zipper down my back. His expression is reverent, focused. I can't look away. We're both breathing hard, ragged little pulses that are all I can hear.

My dress pools around my feet, the silk cool against my skin. I step out of it, shifting it to the side. Thank the stars I decided to wear my favorite bra and thong set.

Sean turns me around to face him.

"How are you even real?" he mutters, before kissing me breathless yet again. His hands spark a trail of heat down the bare skin of my arms, over my lace-covered breasts and hips. I undo his shirt as fast as I can, kissing the exposed skin as I go. He kneads my ass with warm, rough hands. Desperately, I clutch at his naked back as he bites my pebbled nipples through the lace of my bra.

He spins me back around, so that I can see us together. I watch him kiss my shoulder, feeling the hot press of his mouth at the same time. Unsteady, I press my palms against the cold glass, gasping a little at the chill. He notices, his eyes lighting up with something I can't quite define.

Sean undoes the clasp of my bra and it falls away, leaving my heavy, aching breasts exposed. I tip my head back onto his shoulder, watching our reflections as he takes them in his hands. He's rough and gentle all at once, stroking, tugging, teasing my nipples, wringing desperate, needy noises from my throat. I reach behind me. My hands frantically scramble at his belt, then under the layers of his clothes, until at last I'm rewarded. He hisses at the smooth slide of my hands up and down the hot length of his cock.

"Jaysus, woman," he grits out. I laugh, turning my head just far enough to steal another kiss from his hungry mouth.

Sean slides one rough hand down, down, down, and then his clever fingers are sliding my thong to the side and stroking to my clit. I cry out as he draws tight circles around it until I'm panting heavily. I grab his hand and drag a finger down to my entrance. Clever boy that he is, he takes the hint and thrusts first one, then two thick fingers inside me. When I clamp down around his fingers, he swears.

"Mala," he manages, "I need to be inside you."

"Hurry up, then," I demand. His laugh is low and precious. I keep up my strokes, feeling him shiver against my back as he digs in his wallet for a condom. He hands it to me and I tease him, taking my time putting it on.

He growls in my ear. "What happened to hurry up?"

"Keeping you on your toes."

"We'll see about that," he says. Holding my thong to the side, he glides smoothly inside me. His hands grip my waist tightly as he thrusts in and out, almost slipping out but then sliding back home. Fuck, that's good. Even the chill of the thick window glass feels good against my hot nipples as he thrusts into me again and again, smooth and hot and perfect.

He slips one hand between me and the window, playing with my clit, doing something with his thumb and forefinger that absolutely wrecks me. I feel it coming on, that buzz all the way down from the tips of of my toes up my thighs and exploding in a shimmer of sensation, and all I can do is call out his name over and over like a prayer. I've barely come down from my orgasm when Sean thrusts into me once, twice and then the wave hits him, too, dragging my name from his lips again and again.

We collapse onto the floor, exhausted. Sean snags a soft blanket from the chaise, casually draping it over the two of us. We lie there in a silence that is surprisingly comfortable. I don't have anywhere to be, and from the way he's lying here, casually stroking my ass, eyes closed, neither does he.

But. Don't want to overstay my welcome. I lean over and graze his lips with my own, then get up. I need to find my bra. I think it's tucked under the chair —

"Looking for this?" He asks, holding up the offending article.

His voice is even deeper somehow. That relaxed, lazy rumble is almost too low to hear.

"I am, thank you." I reach for it, but he holds it over my head. "Why do you — "

"I suspected you might cut and run." His grin is all lazy arrogance. It's stupid hot. "But there's still the matter of dinner."

Before I can reply, my stomach growls, loudly. That smile of his gets even wider. A blush heats my cheeks.

"If you don't want to be seen with me, there's always room service." He bends down and kisses me again.

"You're annoying."

"I prefer persistent."

"Fine. You're persistently annoying." I kiss him back. "Now can I have my bra?"

"Are you staying for dinner?"

I sigh, digging around in my purse for a hair tie. "Yes. Order something with vegetables. I'm gonna go use up all your hot water."

"I'll join you in five." At my raised eyebrow, he scoffs. "Do you think I'm gonna miss the opportunity to get you in the shower, lass? What am I, mad?"

This man. I don't know exactly what we've started, but I can already tell it's gonna be one hell of a ride.

"Come with me," I plead. I grab a towel and step out of the shower. "Do you want me to beg?"

"Under other circumstances," Mala tells me, a naughty gleam in her eye, "that would be delightful. But honestly, Sean, I don't have time to go to Ireland this month."

While I dry off, I'm watching her do a complicated thing with her hair, turning a trio of braids into some kind of Gordian knot. The red highlights are gone since the last time I saw her. They've been switched out for a warm shade of caramel that makes her hair look like candy.

Jesus. Listen to me. What the fuck do I know about hair? The point is, she's gorgeous. If we hadn't just fucked in the shower — it's become our favorite spot — I'd be trying to get her upstairs and into that massive bed so I can mess up this perfectly controlled hairstyle she's created.

"Next month, then." I say, watching her slide back into her yoga pants. I quickly slip on my sweats and a cotton t-shirt.

"Can't. The Good Netizen Awards are next month." I roll my

eyes, which makes her scowl at me. "I know you don't care, Mister-I-build-the-Internet, but events like these are important to my business."

"I care, Mala," I kiss the back of her neck. "That's important to you. I appreciate that you want to be a rockstar in your field. I admire it."

Good." She makes fancy wings with her eyeliner, and slicks sparkly gloss on her mouth.

"But I also care," I say, rubbing her ass for emphasis, "very deeply and very passionately about spending more than four hours at a time together."

"Oh my god, I can't with you. You literal sex fiend." Mala laughingly wiggles out of my grasp. "I'm heading to the lobby. Meet me in the garage in ten."

We've seen each other a few times since the night we met, but we've gotten into the habit of not being seen together. It's not as if we think the paparazzi are after us, exactly. Still, a surprising number of people keep an eye on my comings and goings. Besides which, Mala's Instagram channel is extremely popular, and she gets recognized often, especially here in town. The last thing she wants is someone connecting her with me. Being known as Sean Reed's... whatever would distract from her own profile.

She wants to keep our private life private. I'm completely on board with that plan. Which is why I suggested that we meet up in Ireland.

It's the perfect spot. We both have 'official' reasons to be there. One of my new projects has a team of developers in Dublin, and it makes sense for me to visit. Mala's entire thing is travel, so she's obviously got the excuse of scouting locations for her viewers. I checked her metrics, and I'm sure her channel's viewers aren't coming from there. Meaning the two of us could actually have a proper vacation. We could just...be with each other.

I'm confident that my plan's relatively foolproof. And the

prospect of spending more than an afternoon or evening together is pretty fucking sweet.

I leave the suite, and head for the garage. I'm halfway there when I get a text from Theo, my best mate.

> As much as it pains me to admit this, you were right.

> This weekend is exactly what I needed.

Ha. I'd sent Theo to a weekend retreat, hoping it would help him find his mojo again. Seems like it's working. I write back.

> I'm going to need that recorded and sent to me so I can play it for you the next time you doubt me.

A honk interrupts me. I look up to see Mala standing next to her car.

"Hey, hot stuff," she says, sliding into the driver's seat. "We need to get a move on. I promised my nephew a trip to the trampoline place this afternoon."

"Ah. That explains the double sports bra situation."

She shrugs. "Gotta protect my second- and third-favorite body parts."

I smile at her words, but I'm a little distracted. She's never mentioned a nephew before. She never talks about her family at all.

To be fair, neither do I. This thing between us has been super casual. Deliberately so, on both of our parts. With our complicated schedules, casual makes complete sense.

Last week, though, I was having lunch with my new foundation's lawyers (courtesy of Young Cameron; he was so proud he finally roped me into sitting down with them). We did the usual dance of schmoozing meeting and paperwork, blah blah blah. But a woman walked by with glowing brown skin and a long dark ponytail, and my heart beat a little faster until I saw her face. Perfectly attractive woman — but not the one I wanted to see.

Then two days ago, I attended a charity dinner. It was fine. I managed to pay attention throughout the event, but then the dessert came. Some kind of cake involving citrus and chocolate — which immediately led my obsessed brain to fixate on Mala's perfume. The scent instantly made my cock throb. I started thinking about PhP just to calm myself down. So a few days in Ireland, where we can get our fill of each other, sounds like a damned good idea to me. I just need to convince my reluctant paramour.

Cameron suggested that I let her know I've "'caught feels' or whatever your generation calls it." I told him to get off of my lawn. The cheeky bugger handed me a book on relationships by some lady called Ria Black and said I might learn a thing or two. I started it, at least. But I got to a chapter on vulnerability and decided that was quite enough for now, thanks.

We pull up to a house in the West Hills.

It's fancy. Far nicer than anyplace I ever lived in Glasgow, but old-fashioned in a way that reminds me of buildings there. The grounds of both this place and the neighbors are well-groomed. It's clear that professional attention is regularly paid. This is good. I make a mental note to ask which garden services are the best. Even thinking about hiring someone for house projects is a real kick in the head for a bloke who grew up with a not very successful plumber for a dad.

The agent, a tall brown-skinned woman with striking white braids, comes down to meet us as we get out of the car.

"Mr. Reid," she says, "Lena Jennaux. It's a pleasure to meet you." She glances at Mala, but doesn't ask.

"The pleasure's mine," I reply. "This is Mala Shah. She's —"

Mala interjects. "Just a nosy friend with excellent taste."

"Of course. Welcome. Why don't we all go inside?" The agent

guides us up the walkway, past the manicured shrubs and massive ceramic planters full of fragrant rosemary.

I admire Lena's poker face. She didn't even blink at Mala's description of her status. Probably comes with the territory. Someone who sells houses likely sees a bit of everything. But I don't think I agree that she's just a friend. Things between us are more intense than that, aren't they?

I put my musings to the side as Lena takes us on a tour of the house. I'm charmed by the beamed ceilings, the bay windows, the William Morris wallpaper in the dining room, and features like dual staircases. It's Mala who asks the questions about the HVAC, the reliability of Internet, security systems and so forth. I'm amused. Who knew that my glamour girl would turn out to be so surprisingly practical?

The agent leaves us on the deck and excuses herself to give us a moment to talk it over. We both walk over to the railing, admiring the lavish view of the city.

"What do you think?" I ask.

"I think you might not be the greatest at shopping for a house, my friend." The smile she flashes me has a touch of mischief. "I know you're richer than God, Sean, but you really should ask some questions about the basics of how the house works."

"Nah, love. That's what my assistants are for."

"What? Assistants? As in more than one?"

"I run a ridiculously large company — well, I used to, anyway. I couldn't have done that without multiple someones to manage my life. I have to outsource domestic responsibilities so my brain doesn't explode."

Mala shakes her head. "I do not even pretend to understand your life."

I shift over so that I'm standing behind her. "These days, it's simple. If there's a problem, I throw money at it. Problem solved."

"I thought you didn't care about the money."

"It buys convenient things. Like tickets to Ireland." I wrap my arms around her and plant a kiss on her hair. The scent of coconut oil wafts up to me.

She turns around, putting her arms around my neck.

"Sean…"

I distract her with a long, lingering kiss. She responds immediately, her generous mouth so soft and pliable under mine. I can never get enough. She presses closer, like she's ready to climb me. I love it.

"Wait, wait," she says, breaking it off. "Let's stick to the issue of the house. Do you even need this much space?"

"Why not? People come to visit. It's always good to have space for that."

"So you're not planning to have a passel of children running around here?"

That pulls me up short. I haven't thought about kids. Kids means permanence. 'Settling down.' That's not where my head's at. I didn't think hers was either, but now I'm curious.

"Do you want kids?"

"This isn't about me." Mala's smile is smug. "I'm asking if this house makes sense for the life you want to lead. Why not a sleek bachelor pad in the Pearl instead?"

"If I buy one of those, will you go on this trip with me?"

"How do we keep ending up back here? Why is this trip such a big deal?"

Maybe that Ria Black is right. A bit of radical honesty might be called for here.

"Because, Mala Shah, I like you." I kiss her again, barely grazing her lips. "And before you say it, this isn't about the sex."

"No?"

"No." I stare into her rich brown eyes. "As much as I enjoy the sex part of our relationship, I also enjoy the talking part. The dinner eating part. The working silently in the same room part. The not kissing my arse because you want something from me part. I need more of that in my life.

"I want to know you, Mala. Not just because you're the woman I'm sleeping with, but because you're a person I think is pretty damned cool."

"You are so annoying," she says, caressing my cheek with her hand. "Just when I think I've got you figured out, you show me a whole other side."

"I'm full of sides. I'm a dodecahedron's worth of sides."

She sighs, but her eyes are soft with emotion. "I'll move some things around. I've always wanted to see Ireland."

Mala

I'm not nervous, I tell myself. *I'm excited. Restless. With perhaps a soupçon of panic. Seasoned with a faint hint of nausea.*

Okay. Maybe I'm nervous.

It makes sense to be nervous. This is A Big Freaking Deal.

It's not every day that a travel network reaches out to you. We were flattered to be noticed. But to specifically request that we pitch ways we can work together? It's a literal dream come true.

Cara, Siobhan and I have been working on FortyFab for five years now. Our views and engagement are consistently great; our ad revenue and merch sales are fabulous. We make good money. But a relationship with a network could expand our audience tremendously. This is a major chance to level up.

"Mala, I need you to sit down," Siobhan orders gently. "You're making me dizzy."

"Sorry, Vonnie," I mutter. "I really want this to go well."

"Of course you do. But wearing a hole in the carpet won't make it any better."

Siobhan, for all her outward calm, is a little excited, too. She's lived in America for more than a decade, but when she gets nervous, her accent gets much stronger. She sounds even sweeter and more charming than usual with Ireland in her voice.

Even thinking the word Ireland conjures up Sean and the trip we just took.

That week was the most incredible experience. I can't even describe it. Travel has been my job for so long, I'd forgotten it could be enjoyable, too.

We stayed in a literal castle, just a little way outside of Dublin. I'd no idea there were so many of these littering the Irish countryside. Trust Sean to find the most extra accommodation possible.

I'm lucky that I get to stay at a lot of really fabulous places, and I encourage women to treat themselves to luxury. This place, though, was on a whole other level. There was a stunningly good spa on site, of course, and multiple restaurants that should be Michelin-starred. But between the clay shooting and archery, the horseback riding and the falconry, even my jaded self was impressed.

The best part of the trip, though, wasn't any of that. It was discovering that waking up next to a sexy Scot who makes it his mission to please you in every way possible is a solid life choice.

I lost count of how many times I woke with his head between my thighs, halfway to an orgasm. Or how rarely we made it to the bed. Against the wall, outside, over the arm of the couch...I've been back in Portland for two days, and I am still pleasantly sore in certain places.

Even better than the sex, we had time for actual conversations. We talked about everything. About our families — his sisters and mom, my parents and sister — about books we love, favorite sports, just any and everything. Not every conversation was super deep or whatever, but it was real.

The night before we left, Sean said, "I know we've been

keeping it simple between us. Relaxed. But what do you think about taking it a little more seriously?"

"What does more seriously look like?"

"I don't know. I've never wanted to find out before. But I want that with you."

My phone buzzes. It's Sean, of course. It's like he knows I'm thinking of him.

Knock 'em dead, lass. I tuck it away, but my smile is impossible to hide. It feels like we reached a new understanding. Like we're making room in our lives to mean something to one another.

"What's got you looking like that cat that swallowed the canary, Mala?" Vonnie's voice snaps me out of my reverie.

"Nothing," I fib. "Just a really good memory." Her skepticism comes out in a weighty grunt, which of course makes me think of Sean again.

"Not anything to do with a certain Scottish tech bro, now would it?" Cara teases.

Before I can answer, an alert pops up on my tablet, and we start the video call. The VP of Programming introduces herself and her team, I introduce Vonnie and Cara, and we're off.

I talk about our mission. How we're dedicated to female travelers and their needs. Siobhan shares metrics on engagement and the community that we've built. Cara wows them with stunning location shots that don't look like anyone else's, and some of the brand partnerships we've developed over time.

I close with a few different ideas on how we can partner: short bumpers wrapped around their existing shows, half hour specials on women and travel, and ultimately, a series of our own.

"I'm impressed," the VP tells us. "This is exactly the kind of multimedia synergy we need to create to position this network more firmly in the 21st century."

"That's great," I say, careful to keep my tone casual. Out of the camera's view, I squeeze Cara and Vonnie's hands.

"Would you like us to send you the deck?"

"Sure. Although I think we've heard enough to say that this feels like a good fit." She looks at her staff for confirmation. They all nod.

"My team will draw up a proposal for an initial run on those bumpers. We should have a draft of the contract to your agent by the end of next week."

Holy shit. I couldn't have asked for a better response if I'd written it myself.

"Fantastic. Looking forward to seeing it."

We say our goodbyes and walk across the room before we squeal.

"We did it, ladies." My voice is shaking, but I don't care. I'm so proud I could explode.

"We did!" Cara's normally quiet expression is gone, replaced with utter glee.

"That was amazing." Siobhan says. "You were amazing. Smooth as silk."

"Not just me. It was all of us. We kicked ass."

We talk a few minutes more, and plan to meet up for a celebratory lunch in about an hour. Cara and Siobhan head off, and I get back to my computer to send over the deck as promised.

When I get back to my desk, I'm hearing a persistent whisper. Suddenly I realize it's coming from the window for the video meeting, which I forgot to close.

"...was right about them," the VP's voice says. "Their work should fit in nicely with our plans for next year. Glad we took the meeting."

"How did you hear about them, anyway? Social media influencers didn't strike me as your demo."

"Reid recommended them to me."

"Sean Reid? As in internet mogul Sean Reid?"

"Yep."

"Huh. Since when is travel his area of interest?"

"Since he bought ten percent of this company."

~

Four hours later, I'm back home on my couch, whiskey in hand. I have no idea how I managed to get through the celebration dinner with Cara and Vonnie. Probably all the alcohol. I'm tipsy enough that I'm floating along on a little cloud, quietly observing myself, wondering how my heart can literally ache this much and yet my body continues to function.

That ache feels all too familiar. I can't believe I got back on this roller coaster again, knowing the ride only ends in misery.

My doorbell rings. A quick glance at the security confirms what I already know: it's Sean. I buzz him in. Better to get this over with.

"I thought you might be out celebrating with Cara and Siobhan." He breezes into my condo, a bottle of Lagavulin in hand. He sets the whiskey on my counter before joining me on the couch. "But I took a chance, because I really wanted to see you. Turns out a week together was not enough."

Sean takes me in his arms, and my traitorous body responds. For just a moment, I let myself forget. One last time, I soak in the smell and the taste of him, trying to imprint it on my brain and body for the long nights ahead.

"So you've heard." I say, when we finally break apart.

"A little bird may or may not have shared that with me." He looks so pleased with himself. As if butter wouldn't melt in his mouth.

"Congratulations, Mala. I'm proud of you."

"Are you? Proud of me?" My voice cracks. I get up and pace. I have to move or I'll explode.

"Of course. Why wouldn't I be?"

"Or is it more that you're proud of yourself?"

He looks up at that, a little pinched frown between his eyes.

"I'm not sure what you mean," he says cautiously.

"Aren't you? Because I think you should be extremely proud of how you managed to ruin something I've been working toward for five years like it wasn't anything at all."

"Ruin it? How on earth —?"

"Did you talk to the travel network about my channel?"

"Sure I did, but—"

"Before or after you gave them millions of dollars?"

I watch the penny drop in real time. Realization spreads across his face that I know what he's done.

"I'm so sorry, Mala. It never occurred to me —"

"Of course not. It wouldn't. You warned me, and I didn't listen. You see a challenge, and you throw money at it. But this wasn't just any challenge, Sean. This was my dream."

He starts to interject, but I keep going.

"For just a minute, I tasted victory. It made all these years of work, all the airports and the lost luggage and the daily posting and the late nights worth it. And then you came along, and put your bazillionaire thumb on the scale, and now no matter what we do, it's not about our merits. It's about the network keeping their big investor happy.

"Now, that victory? It's like ashes in my mouth."

Sean is completely still, except for a clenched jaw he can't quite tame. Those sea glass eyes of his are a desolate, stormy grey.

Despite the ache in my own chest, all I want to do is comfort him. To smooth his furrowed brow, and kiss him until that jumping muscle in his cheek goes away. What the hell is wrong with me?

"You need to go, Sean."

"Mala —"

"This... us... it's never going to work. I need you to go."

He looks at me with such despair in his eyes, I want to take it back. I'll say *never mind, it's fine, I can live with this,* because I'd rather gnaw off my own arm than to cause him even a second of pain. Instead, I take another sip of whiskey and avoid his gaze.

After a moment that feels like eternity, Sean gives me a tight little nod and lets himself out.

I collapse back onto the sofa. I want to cry, but despite that familiar pressure behind my eyes, all I can do is stare at the ceiling.

When the ice shifts in my long-forgotten whiskey, it sounds like the breaking of my heart, all over again. I slug the watered-down scotch in one go.

It's for the best, I tell myself. The scrappy do-it-yourselfer who works ass off, and the man who thinks everything has a price? It was doomed from the start.

But it will be fine. *I* will be fine. It's not like I'm in love with hi—

My brain trips up again as I realize that's exactly what it's like.

I'm in love with him, and he betrayed me. How on earth am I supposed to survive that?

Sean

PRESENT DAY

When I walk into the restaurant, I immediately spot Theo and Aesha nestled together in a corner booth. They're not even touching, but even a stranger could tell there's something special between them. Their bodies subtly angle toward each other, like they're aware of one another right down to a subatomic level. I'd never admit it, but a pang of something very much like jealousy hits me, seeing them like this.

It's not that I begrudge them the happiness they share. I couldn't. Theo is my best mate, one of my favorite people ever. The man's a middle school headmaster, for goodness' sake. He should be canonized for that alone. But I respect him even more because he lost his wife a few years ago, and he didn't crumble in the face of that pain. He managed to thrive, in spite of it, and eventually found love again.

His bravery in taking that plunge a second time — I can't help but admire that.

And Aesha, his lovely fiancée, is utterly perfect for him. She's a brilliant attorney who helps make the world a little bit better on a daily basis. She doesn't take any shit and can kick ass without leaving a mark. But when it comes to Theo, she's absolutely tender. I couldn't have chosen a better partner for him if I tried — and there was a fair bit of trying on my part. Which means that now that they've found each other, and are taking the plunge, I'm all in on the wedding festivities. Including this planning meeting for their bachelor and bachelorette party. I just hope Mala can stand me long enough to get through it.

Do not think about her now, I order myself. It's useless: my brain immediately floods with memories of last night. Mala's hair, spread out across the sheets. Her long, long legs wrapped around my back. Her throaty cries as she came around my cock.

I should've said no when she demanded that I come to her place last night. The last thing we need is for Aesha and Theo to find out that the maid of honor and the best man are... whatever we are. But I can't bring myself to regret a single moment.

I reach the table and shake hands with Theo, some elaborate ritual he's learned from one of his students and taught me. Aesha shakes her head at our silliness, then pulls me in for a hug. A puzzled expression crosses her face, but is quickly smoothed over when the waiter comes by and takes our coffee order. When he leaves, Aesha turns to me.

"So. Sean. How long have you been sleeping with my sister?"

"What — I — How?" I sputter. Theo's brows tick up slightly, while Aesha's expression is smug. I'm busted.

"You smell like her," she tells me. Too late, I remember that I showered before I left Mala's place — with her specially blended soap. Crap. Who knew the bloody stuff would give me away?

But that's partly down to Aesha, too. The woman's so clever, she ought to be a damned private eye.

The arrival of our coffee saves me from the interrogation for now, but I know it's only a brief reprieve. I pull out my phone to send Mala a warning text — I don't want her to walk into this meeting-turned-ambush blind — but Aesha swipes it from my hands before I can even get the messaging app open. Theo barely manages to keep a straight face.

When the waiter's gone, Aesha folds her hands together over her legal pad and turns her full attention on me.

"Spill it," she orders.

"Respectfully, Aesh, I don't think it's really your business —"

"Don't even try it, Sean." Her tone is soft, but no nonsense. "Theo's your best friend, and Mala's my sister. Even beyond the wedding, we're all going to be in each other's lives for a very long time. Spill."

She's right. The mess between Mala and me is exactly the kind of lingering drama that no one wants to be involved in. Especially at our age. We're old enough to know better. We should be, at least.

"We started seeing each other year and a half ago," I tell them. They do the good cop, bad cop thing: Theo quirks a single eyebrow at me while Aesha whispers something in Hindi and rolls her eyes.

I continue. "It was very casual. Things were going great, we took a trip together—"

"Oh, Sean. Dude. You're the fuckboy!" Theo blurts out.

"What?" Both Aesha and I give him a look.

"Aesha, don't you remember that time Mala came for dinner, and we were talking about setting her up with someone from your office?"

Aesha smacks her forehead. "Right!"

"Aesha asked her if she was seeing anyone," he turns toward me. "Mala said absolutely not. She told us the last guy she was with was, and I quote, 'a stupid rich fuckboy who put her off men.' She said her emotions were in a deep freeze."

"Right!" Aesha nods. "And then I tried to figure out if she meant stupid rich like wealthy, or stupid comma rich which is a different thing altogether —"

"Okay, I get the picture, thanks." Jeez. They say you should never find out what people say about you when you're not in the room. I'm starting to see why.

"What did you do to her?" Aesha asks me. Her face is carefully neutral. Still, that protective big sister vibe in her voice is unmistakable. I've heard it often enough from my own sisters to recognize that tone.

"A good thing. Or so I thought."

"So good she dumped you?" Theo asks.

"Teddy Bear. You're my best mate. Aren't you supposed to be on my side?"

He shrugs, noncommittal. I can't blame him. He loves me, but Mala's about to be his sister-in-law. He cares about her, too. I sigh.

"I made the mistake of mentioning her work to a business associate of mine."

Aesha and Theo stare at me, the same disbelieving expression on their faces. I sip my coffee. Theo starts to speak, but Aesha puts a gentle hand on his arm. My eyes swivel back and forth between then while they have an entirely silent conversation.

His look asks *You sure?* While hers says *Yep. I got this, love.* His is very much *Go on then.*

Aesha whips out a scrunchie from somewhere and scrapes her hair back into a bun. When she slips on her glasses and pulls out a legal pad, I get a tad nervous. I'm pretty sure I'm about to be lawyered within an inch of my life.

"Sean," she begins, looking over the top of her lenses, "Our wedding is extremely important to me. We want and need and deserve for this to be a good day."

I swallow hard. My conscience is already pricking me fiercely.

"I'm sure you can understand why these... shenanigans between you and Mala are a problem." She makes a note on her legal pad. I look over, but I can't read her writing upside down.

"So I'd like you to clear this up for me. Let me see if I understand: You mentioned my sister's channel to a business associate, and now she's furious with you."

"Yes."

"Although not too furious for hate sex."

"Yes."

"Okay. That means you've done something dumb, but probably not unforgivable." Before I can interject, she continues.

"Who was this business associate?"

"Lila Owens."

"Lila Owens, as in the Vice President of Programming at The Traveler's Network?"

"Yes." Is it hot in here? I reach for one of the many glasses of water on the table.

"And what was your goal in mentioning Mala's work to Ms. Owens?"

"It was just chit-chat. Networking. Small talk." She's relentless. I feel like I'm on the witness stand. I look at Theo, but he's no help. He's watching her question me with a lovestruck look on his face. The man's hopeless.

"Small talk. With the programming director of the travel network. The same travel network in which you invested a substantial sum of money."

"Mala was the only reason I even looked into the travel market," I say. "Learning about her channel got me interested in it, so I investigated. I thought it had growth potential, so I made an investment."

"And of course, you told Lila what got you interested."

"I did. They asked, I answered. It was just idle conversation."

Theo jumps in. "I know this is hard to understand because you didn't grow up with a lot—"

"How is that relevant?" I grit out. Embarrassment swamps me, tightening my chest and speeding up my pulse. Huh. You'd think I'd be over it by now, considering how much my financial situation has changed, but apparently I'm still a little bit broken.

"Still, Sean." Theo taps my shoulder, kindly ignoring my flushed face and obvious discomfort. "You have to play this out to the end. You're extremely wealthy now, and you don't even realize the power that gives you."

"Power? What power, Theo?" I'm annoyed, and I let it seep into my voice. "The power to be stared at almost everywhere I go? The power to be gossiped about in the media? The power to have people treat you differently because they always want something from you? That's not power. It's a freaking nightmare."

"Sean." Aesha takes off her glasses. Her voice is kinder, softer. "You might not have meant it that way, but money talks. And yours did a lot of talking."

"So merely mentioning FortyFab while I was doing this deal came off like I was trying to buy my girlfr — like I was buying Mala a job?" They nod. My gut churns. "For fuck's sake. I can't even make a casual comment without people thinking I have an ulterior motive."

"Is that what you were doing?"

"Absolutely not. Why would I try to buy her a job when she'd already built a successful career? She didn't need me to prop her up."

Aesha's phone buzzes. She looks at it, mouths "it's Riz" to Theo and excuses herself. I catch a faint "What's up, beta?" as she walks away. Theo smiles as he watches her go. He loves Aesha's son nearly as much as he does her.

"Did you explain the misunderstanding to Mala?"

"I tried, but she kicked me out. Went down like a cup of cold sick."

Theo grimaces. "Dude. I am forever scarred by that expression."

"Seriously, Theo. What do I do? How do I fix this?"

"Try apologizing again? I don't know. You had to help me figure things out with Aesha, remember? But you're the smartest man I've ever met. I trust you to figure it out."

While I appreciate his confidence, Theo's faith in me feels misplaced.

It's going to take everything I have just to get through this wedding planning without wrecking the delicate truce Mala and I have now. If I want to make sure it all goes perfect for Aesha and Theo, the best thing I can do is put my feelings on hold until this is all over.

Then I'll see if there's any way to melt the ice around Mala's heart.

Cara, Siobhan and I are sitting in Cara's van, watching the dailies.

"And that's the real story behind the delicious maraschino cherry. I'm Mala Shah, and this is FortyFab on The Traveler's Network."

I don't love listening to my own voice — it sounds much better in my head — but I've gotten used to it over the last few years.

"It's a good take." Vonnie declares.

"There's not too much wind in the background?" I turn to Cara.

"There's a little, but it's good. Gives it that woman-on-the-street feel. Well, woman in the middle of a cherry orchard, but you know what I mean. TTN will love it."

I give her a quick thumbs up as I swipe the makeup from my face. I've almost learned to ignore the pinch of my conscience whenever the network comes up.

Speaking of my conscience, my phone buzzes with a reminder to confirm the floral order for Aesha's bachelorette party. I send the florist an email.

I've kinda been on my sister's shit list since she found out about Sean and me. All I saw was a cryptic text from him — apparently Aesha snatched his phone away before he could warn me, and "Ah shite" was all he managed to write. So guess who blithely walked right into the world's most awkward brunch just after he confessed? Whew. The bottomless mimosas were mandatory that day.

I know we should've said something months ago, but it never seemed like the right time. Besides, it's not the kind of thing you just announce. "Hey, sis, FYI: had a fling with your guy's BFF. Just thought you should know!" Not even Emily Post knows the etiquette for that situation.

Besides, our thing ended before Aesha and Theo really got serious. After Sean pulled that stunt with the network, I was sure we were done. I figured we'd see each other in passing, a few times a year at best.

And then he found me at their engagement party. I was still furious, of course. But there he stood, looking all kinds of delicious, and me — I was weak. So I took him home and let him have his way with me and even now, I don't regret a single moment.

"Hey, Mala." Vonnie taps me on the shoulder. "Maybe come back down to earth with the rest of us?"

"Not to pile on, babe, but you've been really scattered these days." Cara adds. "Is it Aesha's wedding?"

"Nothing. It's fine. I'm fine. Let's just go."

Cara and Siobhan exchange a look, but they acquiesce and we drive back into town. We make plans for our next batch of interstitials — we're going down the West Coast, which should give us enough material to finish out the year. We're focusing on more international trips for our own channel.

"We might try Ireland," Siobhan offers. "I'd like to go see my mum. Enjoy some old-fashioned Irish hospitality. There's nothing like it."

"That sounds nice," I reply. "Maybe somewhere on the other coast this time. I'd like to see how different it is."

When neither of them responds, I look up. Cara's pulling into a parking spot near Columbia Park.

"What are we doing?" I ask.

"Neutral territory," Cara announces. I'm baffled. Neutral territory means serious team discussion. Doesn't matter where we talk, just that it can't be at any of our homes.

The three of us get out and head into the park. The crunch of needles beneath our feet and the sharp smell of pine is soothing. A group of kids plays near the splash pad, although it's too cool for it to be on. I envy them. Wouldn't it be nice if I could just leave the adult responsibilities behind and play like them?

"Mala, hon," Siobhan says. "You've been lying to us."

I wince. She's right. I didn't know it was that obvious. But these two are my closest friends as well as being my business partners. If anyone outside of my family knows me, it's them.

"When did you go to Ireland, love?"

Cara jumps in. "And more importantly, do you want to end our partnership with TTN?"

"Why do you ask?"

"Because every time we mention them, your face closes up. You just go blank." Cara tucks a blond curl back into her ponytail. I look at Siobhan, who nods. "If you're unhappy, you need to speak up."

Damn it. Not only have I been lying to my sister and Theo, I've been lying to my best friends as well. What a mess.

"I am unhappy," I admit. I take a deep breath. "But not for the reasons you might think."

I tell them the whole sordid story. About my trip to Ireland and what I thought was happening between Sean and me — as well as what I overheard Lila Owens and her team discussing, and Sean's admission that he bought our way into this deal.

"I'm sorry for keeping this from you," I say. "I know I should have told you sooner."

They both squeeze my hands, warming my jaded little heart. No idea how I got so lucky to get these two in my life. I don't deserve them.

"I was angry and embarrassed. I couldn't believe someone I lo — someone I cared about would undermine me like that."

Both Cara and Siobhan are silent for a while. We keep walking through the park, watching the kids and the squirrels and just being together. It reminds me of the walking meditation another friend recommended to me. This walk has a similar effect: I feel surprisingly lighter. Or maybe that's just the relief of my conscience.

"Hon," Cara says. Her hazel eyes are gentle and earnest. "Not to take his side, but — are you sure Sean meant to buy your way into the network?"

She notices my frown, but keeps going. "Maybe — just maybe — he was trying to be supportive. Showing off his knowledge of the sector. TV is an old-fashioned medium. Adding our content is moving the channel into the modern media landscape much faster than they could do on their own."

I start to protest, but hold back. Cara's been my friend for more than a decade. Unlike certain other people in my past, she wouldn't bullshit or gaslight me about this. For the first time, I seriously consider the possibility that Sean only wanted to help.

"Our segments have been extremely popular with TTN viewers. Viewership is up twenty five percent on their shows that include us." Siobhan adds, pulling up a report on her phone. I have to laugh. Trust her to have the stats handy.

"Not to mention that both FortyFab's and TTN's followers have nearly doubled in the time that we've been working together. The network wants to move up the timetable for a show of our own. That wouldn't be happening if we sucked."

"So even if your boyfriend got us in the door," Cara says, "his money couldn't keep us there if our work didn't speak for itself."

"Yep," Siobhan agrees. "Long story short, you should've told us. Then we could've let you know what an idiot you were being sooner."

Cara's voice is soft when she says "Not everyone is like Peter, you know."

Her words hit like a hammer, and for a second, my chest feels like it's collapsing in on itself. That joyous experience is the legacy of Peter Neill, my utterly toxic mess of an ex. The one who love bombed me, made me fall for him, then dumped me when he got a job with a big media company. He claimed they "wanted to go in a different direction" with the show that he and I had built together. I wasn't good enough to come work there with him, but it didn't stop him from stealing my concept and literal year of hard work.

"Cara," Siobhan chides, "I thought we agreed never to bring up the Internet's Biggest Arsehole."

I bark out a shaky laugh, grateful to have these two by my side. They always know the exact right thing to say.

"Oh, man. This has been killing me for so long. I wanted to tell you both, but —"

"You didn't want us to doubt ourselves or question our abilities." Siobhan crosses her arms over her chest.

"Projection much?" Cara's smile eases the sting of her words.

"Wow, dial it back. No one signed up for this much honesty so early in the day," I complain.

"Oh, please. You know this honesty is why we're friends." Vonnie's smile turns smug. "So no more gloomy Gussie, eh?"

"No more, promise."

"Now. What are you gonna do about that handsome lad?"

"There isn't anything to do about him, Vonnie." I shrug. "I think... I think we had a moment. But it passed. End of story."

Cara pats my arm. "Maybe, maybe not. If you both want it, who says you can't make a new moment?"

I appreciate their optimism, even if I don't share it. Whatever existed between Sean and me, it's over. Even if he only meant to help, the fact that a word from him could literally change the course of my career...I can't be vulnerable like that. FortyFab is too important to me.

There will be no more moments. I'll just have to get over the man I love.

Sean

onight has to be perfect.

Theo and Aesha are counting on me — on us — to make it so.

They wanted a masked ball, of all things. Something about masks being a 'theme' in their relationship. I decided discretion was the better part of valor and didn't ask questions. Best not to get ideas in my head that I'll want to bleach out later.

As the man and woman of the hour, their wish was our command. So Mala and I came together to make it happen. For weeks, we've picked out flowers, matched colors, and even did menu tastings.

Considering that it was the first time the two of us had ever worked together — and that neither of us knew what we were doing — I think we did a fine job. The ballroom looks fantastic.

The best part of organizing this party, though, was spending time with Mala. There's been something different about her in the last few weeks. For one, she insisted on working directly with me. I'd offered to have Cameron help so she didn't have to deal with our baggage. Shockingly, she demanded that I be the one to put in the work, or it wouldn't count. For another, I've caught her looking at me like... it's ridiculous, I know, but it's almost like Mala's kicking my tires. She hasn't said any such thing, but if there's the slightest chance for us, I'll do whatever it takes.

To prove it, I threw myself into the planning. I showed up early to every meeting. I tried on the masks to make sure they're comfortable. I sampled half the hors d'oeuvres menu to make sure they weren't drippy or messy. I even took dancing lessons so I'd be able to get people on the dance floor. With every action, I'm trying to show her I am all in. If she's willing to give us another try, to put up with my bizarre life, I'll jump in with both feet.

I adjust my bow tie, feeling faintly ridiculous. Sure, I wear a suit most days, but a tux is a whole other level of torture. Hopefully, once the drinks start flowing, this party will get less formal and I can lose this annoying knot around my neck.

I check in with the bandleader, confirming the order of events, when his eyes dart away from me and nearly pop out of his head. I turn around to see what's got him so discombobulated.

Mala is framed in the doorway, and she looks magnificent.

Her hair is pinned up in one of those amazing braided styles she does: it looks like a crown around her head. Her makeup is flawless. Somehow it manages to play up her cheekbones and emphasize her bold, dark eyes. Her mouth is coated in a bold plum that makes me want to lick it. Even so, it's the gown that turns my brain inside out.

The skirt is a deep, rich blue, shot through with sparking gold threads that make it shimmer. It's overlaid with almost architectural gold stitching that looks like a cityscape. The upper portion of the gown is a cropped halter, covered in the same stitching on a smaller scale, that leaves her arms and her midriff bare. She's also got a sheer wrap with bright flowers stitched into its fabric draped over her head and upper arms.

I've seen Mala naked, clothed, and everything in between, but I've never seen her look like a goddess before.

My mouth goes dry, watching her hips sway as she crosses the room toward me. She's dazzling. Magnetic. I'm pulled toward her like an iron filing.

I gesture at her. "This is…majestic. It suits you."

Mala spins in front of me, ending in a graceful curtsy and a sultry laugh that goes straight to my cock.

"Thank you." She scans me from head to toe. Bites her lip. Moves in closer. "You look pretty good yourself."

We haven't touched each other since the night of the engagement party. My need for her is a physical ache. I know this isn't the perfect moment, but I can't wait.

Just as I reach for her, the door creaks and a tall, brown-skinned man who looks like a cartoon prince come to life waltzes in the door. Mala gasps and runs to him, throwing herself into his arms. A pit of jealousy opens up and swallows me whole as he picks her up and spins her around. Resentment burns in my gut as he laughs and smiles, squeezing her close.

"Nikhil! When did you get back?"

"Yesterday." He smiles down at her with his bloody handsome face and plants a kiss on her forehead. "I couldn't miss didi's big party, could I?"

"How long are you staying?" Mala glances over at me, as if she's only just recalled my existence. She gestures for me to come over. I do, despite wishing that I were literally anywhere else on the planet.

"Wait, never mind that. We'll talk later. Nik, this is Sean. He's, um, the groom's best friend. Sean, this is my brosin Nikhil Shah."

"Your what now?"

"Technically, we're cousins," Nikhil offers me one of those movie star smiles as we shake hands. "But I basically lived at their house growing up."

"Ah. Brother/cousin, gotcha. Great to meet you." Now that I know he's her relative and not a rival.

"Same, same. Excuse us a moment?" Mala takes his arm and drags him away, a stream of Hindi following in their wake. I get back to my pre-party checklist, conferring with the hotel catering staff. They're more than ready, and my check-in is a formality, but it distracts me from obsessing about the way Mala glows in that dress.

Slowly, Aesha and Theo's guests filter into the ballroom and the party gets underway. Mala and I are on opposite ends of the room for hours, chatting up people and making sure they're fed and watered as needed. I'm pleased to see that people are really into this theme. I'd had my doubts, but the mask thing is a hit.

In fact, wearing my mask all night has been a relief. No one's pointing their phone my way or being weird around me. Which means I feel more normal than I have in a very long time. I wonder if Aesha and Theo did this on purpose. They're lovely like that; I wouldn't put it past them.

"Hey." Mala whispers into my ear. I turn around and am once again gobsmacked by how gorgeous she is. "We did good, didn't we?"

She gestures at Theo and Aesha. They're out on the dance floor leading a group lesson. Fifteen years of friendship, and I had no idea Theo could dance. Hidden depths.

"Yeah, we did." The music changes to something slow and angsty. I hold out my hand. Mala looks at it awkwardly, and I can see the indecision on her face. I awkwardly pull it back.

"I — um — we should talk about the payment for this," she says suddenly.

"No need."

"Sean, this is not an inexpensive event —"

"Mala. It's already been handled."

"You can't just go around doing that." Her voice is low and tight with fury. I don't understand.

"Doing what? Giving my friends a gift?"

"Throwing your money around. It's — it's obnoxious."

"It's hardly throwing my money around. I'm doing something nice for the people I care about."

"Is that what you think this is? Care?" Her eyes are suspiciously bright. "You have a fucked up way of showing it."

"Mala —"

"Don't." She holds up her hand as if to physically restrain me. "I thought maybe you were starting to understand. It was foolish of me to hope."

She adjusts her wrap, tucking one end into a belt around her waist. "Goodbye, Sean."

I grab her hand. "No."

"Is everything alright?" Mala's cousin Nikhil asks. He just appeared out of nowhere. His voice is relaxed, calm even, but there's a protective undercurrent that's impossible to miss. Annoyed as I am at the interruption, I admire how much the Shahs look out for each other.

"We're fine, Nik," she assures him. "You know the thing Uncle-ji does where he steals the check before anyone else can get it? Same same."

His eyebrows lift an infinitesimal fraction. "Ah. A man after my own heart. Respect."

Weirdly, I'm pleased. Mala obviously adores him, which means his approval is a point in my favor.

"Maybe turn down the temperature though, Mala? You look like you're about to throw your glove in his face and demand satisfaction."

She blushes a little. "Got it. We should take this outside."

"Outside is an excellent idea," I agree quickly. "Let's go."

I grab Mala's hand and head for the doors. I know she won't make a scene, especially not after she reassured her cousin that all was well. It's petty, but I never claimed to be better than that.

When we make it past the gauntlet of guests and out the door, Mala drops my hand like a hot rock and drags me into a small alcove off to the side.

"Ugh, you are so annoying," she rants. "Can you please just stop?"

"Stop what?"

"Stop acting like your money is the answer to every single problem."

Ah. There's the rub. Briefly, bitterness grips me in a chokehold. The one thing I thought was an asset has turned out to be anything but. I flash back to that book Cameron gave me, to the chapter on vulnerability that I tried to skip. If this relationship is gonna have a chance, that kind of honesty is what Mala needs from me.

"You remember, when we were in Ireland, I told you a little about my childhood, yeah?" She nods. "What I hid between the lines was that I grew up poor as a church mouse."

She's startled, but still open. I keep talking.

"My whole life, I wanted enough money to help my family and friends. I thought it would fix everything. Then I made that much, and more besides. It felt like a miracle. Now, it's the worst form of irony that the thing I wanted most in life is the thing standing between me and the woman I can't live without."

She gasps, covering her mouth with her hand. We stare at each other, and I can almost see her pushing back at the tide of feelings. Despite her best efforts, a tear slides down her face. I pull her into my arms and try to put every ounce of what I feel for her in our embrace.

"Mala," I say. She tips her head up to look at me. "I know you think I didn't trust your ability to get the job, but that's the farthest thing from the truth. It's because of your work that I even thought to invest in TTN.

"You're brilliant, and I would never disrespect you by trying to buy you a job. You don't need that from me. You're enough — more than enough — all on your own."

I kiss her then. I can't help it. I need her to understand what she means to me.

She hesitates at first, but then I feel her give in to the kiss. She tastes like every dream I've ever had. Everything I've ever wanted in life, all right here.

When we break apart, she gently presses at my chest. Reluctantly, I let her go. She puts a little distance between us, and I hate it.

"FortyFab is my baby. My friends and I, we built this thing that nobody believed in except us. Social media was new and fickle and how could it possibly bring in enough revenue to support an entire crew? It was madness. We were insane to think it could work.

"But it did. We made it work. And it's precious to me. I can't put it at risk because of my relationship with you."

"Mala, I love you." My voice breaks on the words, but I've never meant anything more. "I'd never hurt you or your company."

"I know you wouldn't mean to."

"Then what on earth is the problem?"

"What do I do when you stop, Sean?" She's crying freely now. "What happens when you stop loving me?"

"That will never, ever happen."

"You can't know that. You feel one way now, but things change. People change." She wipes away a tear. "And if I lost you, if you stopped loving me, it would hurt like fuck and I'd be miserable. But to be miserable *and* lose the thing I've worked so hard for? It would break me."

"Is that the kind of man you think I am? That I'd take away something you built?"

"You wouldn't be the first."

"I would never." My fists clench at my sides; I deliberately force myself to relax. I make a mental note to find whoever the bastard is that hurt her and kick every inch of his arse. But that pleasure will come later. Right now, I need to show her how committed I am to this. To us.

"I'm still uncomfortable being the richest guy in the room. I don't know to billionaire properly, and I'd never want to. I never want to stop being as normal as I can be.

"I didn't know my power in this situation, or how it would look. But what I do know is that you amaze and impress me every single day. And if what you need is for me to stay away from your work, then I'm happy to comply."

I pull an envelope out of my inner pocket and hand it to her.

She opens it and gasps when she reads the papers.

"Oh my god." Her face is a study in confusion. "These are —"

"All the shares in TTN that I owned," I confirm. "They're yours now."

Mala starts to reply, but I keep going.

"Keep 'em, donate 'em to charity, doesn't matter. They're unrestricted, and they're one hundred percent yours."

"I — I don't know what to say." Her eyes flit from me to the paper and back again. "This is unbelievable."

"I'm telling you, lass: I am absolutely crazy about you. That means I want you to be happy. I want you to feel safe. I will turn the world upside down to make that happen. You deserve nothing less."

I squeeze her hand, and then walk away. It's the hardest thing I've ever had to do in my life. But I know it's right. If she does come to me, it has to be her choice. No strings, no coercion.

I'm almost at the door when I hear her call out "Wait!" I turn around.

"This is the kindest thing anybody's ever done for me," she says, voice trembling but still strong. "I didn't know that I could be loved like that. You're right. I do deserve it. And so do you."

She practically runs into my arms and throws herself at me. If I thought our last kiss was like a bonfire, this one is an inferno.

"Sean," she whispers in my ear. Fuck. That throaty sound goes straight to my cock. "I need you."

I push her back into that darkened alcove. Her breathing gets ragged when I set her down on the ledge and hike up her skirt. Her legs gleam in the half light, but I'm wholly focused on what's between them.

I pull up a chair and get to work.

The first swipe of my tongue against her fever hot pussy wrings a moan from her throat. I grab her ass and scoot in closer to get a better angle. I slip my thumbs underneath the edge of her crop top and stroke her nipples, feeling them harden beneath my determined touch.

All the while, I'm teasing her clit with my tongue, relishing the taste of her, until she's gripping my hair with both hands and gasping for breath. I'm relentless, working nipples and sucking her clit until she comes with a sob, my name on her lips like a prayer.

I slip my arms around her, holding her until the aftershocks subside.

"Will that hold you, then?" I tease. She looks at me quizzically, big brown eyes still half-dazed with lust. "We really ought to get back to the party."

"That'll do for now," she whispers, kissing me deeply. "But you know I'll need more later."

She quickly sets herself to rights, and we head for the door.

"How do I look?" she asks.

Like the woman I'm going to marry, I think.

Out loud, I simply say "Perfect."

Mala

TWO MONTHS LATER

I'm setting the table when I overhear Sean grousing.

"Tell me why I didn't hire someone to do this again?"

No matter how often I hear it, that burr in his voice immediately makes my thighs clench. I try to get my mind out of the gutter, since it's utterly inappropriate for the occasion, but it doesn't matter. Everything about him is sexy as hell, and his voice in particular makes me weak in the knees.

"It was your idea not to," Cameron reminds him. "Something about building character, doing some things for yourself? I wasn't really listening. Hand me that cable, please."

I smile to myself. Cameron continues to excel at keeping his grumpy boss in line. I mean, I have my own ways, but most of those involve getting naked. I might have to ask his assistant for some non-sexy tips.

The doorbell rings. When I answer it, my sister, future brother-in-law and darling nephew come barreling in. Cara and Siobhan are close behind.

"Happy housewarming, Auntie," Riz tells me, handing over a gorgeous vase with an enormous air plant inside.

"It's about time you're the one giving me gifts," I tell him. He rolls his eyes. I send him out to the deck, which the other tweens in the family have already staked out as their territory. I direct Cara and Vonnie to the family room so they can wrangle my parents and their siblings for family photos. Nikhil, who's done nothing more than warm one of the dining room chairs until now, jumps up and offers to help them manage our unruly elders.

Sean and Cam have finished their project, and come rolling in with the VR device. His mother and sisters appear in our living room, about life sized.

"And here she is: my beautiful beloved," Sean announces, handing it over to Cameron. He sweeps me into his arms and dips me in a dramatic pose.

"Tavish Sean Reid, you're off your head." His mother's voice is fond and stern all at once. "Stop tossing the lass around like a sack of potatoes."

"Aye, mum." I suppress a smile. His accent always gets broader when he's talking to his family. "Hold on a sec."

He stands me upright and whispers in my ear. "Don't you dare laugh. You know you like it when I toss you around."

Without missing a beat, he goes back to his call. "Let me take you outside and show you the view. It's mad."

"What on earth did Sean say to put that expression on your face?" My sister asks me. When I blush even more deeply, she holds up a hand. "You know what? Never mind. I cannot know that about you two. I'm glad you're happy, though."

Later, after the photos are taken and the food is eaten and our guests have gone home, and we're sitting on our deck, that thought comes back to me. My sister's right. I am happy. In a way I never thought I could be.

"Alright, love?" Sean asks. He kisses my hand.

"With you? Always." We sit in silence for a few minutes, just listening to the night.

A sharp buzz breaks the moment.

"That's my cue," Sean says. He clicks it off. I watch him stretch, shamelessly ogling the man I love. He comes closer to me and gets down on one knee.

"Mala Shah, I've asked you every night for the last two months. And I will ask again until you say yes. Will you marry me?"

Our life together is not what I imagined. Half the time, we're in different cities, states, continents. And when we are in the same place, we're still learning how to be a unit.

But I know in my heart that wherever we are, no matter how far apart, this man is my home. That makes me change my answer.

"Yes."

Sean blinks, like he can't quite believe what he just heard.

"Are you sure, lass?"

"Sir! *You* proposed to *me*!"

"I know, but — I figured I had at least another six months of begging for your hand before you gave in. I was prepared to wait."

"Well, if you don't want to..." I tease.

"Not a chance. I'll have us on a plane to Vegas in an hour."

"Vegas?"

"We can have a fancy splash out later, if that's what you want. But you said yes today." He kisses me breathless. "I'm not taking the chance you'll change your mind."

There's absolutely no chance of that. But I love that he wants this as much as I do.

And a few hours later, slightly dazed, but very, very happy, we start the rest of our lives together.

Bet on Me

Cara

"Get in, loser. We're going to Vegas."

I groan at my best friend's cheesy line. Mala wiggles her eyebrows at me in an exaggerated way as I scoot past her into the leather seated interior of the private plane.

"How long have you been planning that?" I ask her.

She gives me a sneaky grin. "Pretty much since I called you."

I roll my eyes. "Speaking of: please never do that again. You nearly gave me a heart attack! Who calls people anymore?"

"Come on, it was urgent. Would you have believed me if I texted?"

She's got a point. It's a little shocking to think that two hours ago, I was at Mala and Sean's housewarming. Now I'm strapping into a seat on Sean's private plane for a flight to Las Vegas and an impromptu wedding.

Mala's sworn me to secrecy for several reasons. First and foremost: her sister is marrying Sean's best friend. Those two are going very traditional, doing the whole long engagement and wedding thing, with all the parties and planning and big fuss. The last thing Mala and Sean want is to overshadow those events. They're determined to let Aesha and Theo enjoy the spotlight.

For another thing: Sean's status as a tech billionaire, and Mala's job as a travel show host/influencer, means they're just famous enough to be interesting. When they went public with their relationship, we were all pretty surprised at how many reporters started to track their every move. The two of them hopping on a plane to Vegas would create a crazy amount of speculation.

What the reporters don't know is that Sean has literally proposed to her every day for the last two months. Or that every day, she's told him 'not yet.' I don't know what he did to make her say yes this time, but as she laughingly shared on the phone, he's determined to get them hitched before she comes to her senses.

Although, I think, watching the two of them together, I'm pretty sure neither Sean nor Mala are in their right minds. Anyone who sees them can tell how crazy they are for one another.

I'm happy for them. Even if that happiness is tinged with a little bit of envy. I want that so much. That head over heels, reckless obsession with someone? It's so delicious.

Not that I've experienced it in a relationship. The last guy I dated was... convenient. We got along fine, but who wants fine? I need more.

My personal pity party is interrupted by the opening of the plane door — and the entrance of one Dr. Nikhil Shah.

AKA Mala's cousin. AKA the only man who's ever made me feel that kind of reckless desire. AKA the hottest man I've ever met in my life.

Talk about delicious. Nik looks like a movie star. Dark, curly hair, body like a basketball player, beautiful bronze skin, eyes that glow like obsidian... How could I not lust after him? It would be impossible.

From the second I met him at the tender age of eight, I've been crazy about him. Too bad for me that it's all been one-sided. He's never shown any sign that he thinks of me as anything more than Mala's friend.

Although there was that one time..., my brain insists.

We were at Hotel D for Aesha and Theo's engagement party. Sean and Mala hosted the event, which was a fancy dress masked ball. I wished I had my video camera. There were so many moments I wanted to capture, but my friends insisted that I needed to be a guest instead of working.

I'd just come off the dance floor when I felt... something. I don't know what it was. When I turned around, Nik and I made eye contact across the room. I swear, it was just like a movie. Everyone else in the room faded away as we made our way toward each other.

"Cara." His voice was warm. Promising. He held out a hand.

"Nik. You're back." I put my hand in his, and he took me out onto the floor.

On the surface, everything was normal. We made small talk about my work with Mala on FortyFab, his last assignment in Bangladesh, and his retirement from Doctors Who Care.

But inside, every princess fantasy I ever had roared to life in my brain. Considering the way he was looking at me, I fully expected him to sweep me out of the ballroom and off to a dark corner, where he'd have his wicked way with me. I'd already scoped out half a dozen potential locations.

Instead, when the music ended, Nik gave me a polite smile and patted me on the shoulder.

"Thanks for the dance," he'd said. "And by the way, that's a great dress."

In the two months since then, he might have said ten words to me — and half of those would probably be 'goodbye.' If you looked up taciturn in the dictionary, his picture would be next to it.

Never mind what I thought I saw in his eyes that night. I can take a hint. He's not interested in me as a woman. I'm just the annoying girl next door, all grown up.

Or worse. He doesn't find me annoying. He's simply indifferent to my existence.

If only I could make myself feel the same. But even though it's been thirty years, I've never been able to fully shake this crush. Aside from the movie star looks and being a genius doctor who spends his time caring for people in desperate circumstances, there's a genuine, warm person behind the gruffness. In those rare times when Nik does open up, I see glimpses of that man. I want to spend more time with him. I'm pretty sure that man would be my friend.

Too bad I'll never get to find out for sure.

I clear my throat. "You didn't tell me Nikhil was coming."

"Didn't I?" Mala looks up from her phone, briefly, before turning back to her email. "We wanted two witnesses. Obviously can't ask Theo, so Nik offered to come in his place."

"That's... that's nice of him."

"A free week in Vegas, hanging out with his favorite cousin?" She winks. "What's not to love?"

I glance over at Nik. As usual, he's in a suit. He seems to live in them. I'm not mad at him for that choice. They show off his broad shoulders and well-toned body to perfection.

He gets settled into his seat, e-reader already in his hand. When he looks up and sees me, I get a quick nod before he returns to whatever book he's reading.

Yep. No interest at all. I sigh and pull out my own book. I can tell this is going to be a great week.

The flight from Portland to Las Vegas is fast — about two hours total — and the trip from the airport to the Vegas branch of Hotel D is mere minutes. I don't get much time to see it all, but there's a lot happening on the Strip. I'm fascinated — and a little intimidated, too.

But instead of stopping on the glittering main drag, the limousine turns down a private drive instead. We stop in front of a striking sandy-colored complex of condos with balconies that look out over an enormous golf course. It's beautiful.

As we exit the vehicle, we're met by a young man in a waistcoat and trousers.

"Good evening. Welcome to Hotel D Vegas." he announces. "I'm Cody. I'll be your butler during your stay."

Cody directs his team of porters to take our luggage. Sean and Mala follow the porters one way, and we go another. He gives us a tour of the place. It's essentially a three bedroom luxury apartment, with soothing taupe walls and desert-themed art. The living spaces are dominated by comfortable white leather furnishings, a TV that is bigger than my entire condo, and a collection of enormous potted ferns and Monstera plants. The main bedroom continues the color scheme, with beautiful dark furniture that sharply contrasts with the plush white linens. Its dedicated marble-tiled bath holds an enormous glass-doored shower and a jetted bathtub so big I could practically swim in it. The other two bedrooms, thoughtfully placed down a hall, away from the main bedroom, share an equally ornate bathroom.

There's a bit of awkwardness when the porters start to put both Nik's luggage and mine into the primary suite.

"I — that is, we're not —" I stammer, blushing.

"I'll be sleeping in one of the suites down the hall," Nik steps in to save me from my awkward flailing. "If you could have my things placed there, I'd appreciate it."

"Understood, sir," Cody replies, not blinking an eye.

"You didn't have to give up this room," I say, after they've left us alone. "We could've flipped for it."

"I saw the way your eyes lit up at the sight of that tub," he says with a grin. "I couldn't possibly deny you the pleasure."

I'm this close to making an inappropriate joke about pleasures and denial, which will no doubt make this entire experience extremely awkward. Fortunately, a text from Sean saves me from myself, and the four of us meet up downstairs. Another quick limo ride finds us outside the marriage bureau office.

"Last chance to back out, Mala," Sean warns, tilting his head in the direction of the door. "Then you're stuck with me forever."

"I can't wait," she replies. The look — and kiss — they share is so tender, I have to turn away.

The four of us head into the clerk's office to get the marriage license. Nikhil and I wait on the side, smiling awkwardly at one another while we wait for Sean and Mala. They have a brief conversation with the clerk and get their paperwork completed.

The wedding is spur of the moment, true, and we'll have to keep it hush hush until she and Sean are ready to tell people, but seeing the two of them love each other is honestly inspirational. I want what they have someday. I vow to myself that I won't settle for less.

"Ready?" Sean asks us both, slipping the paperwork into his pocket. I'm startled. I'd been so wrapped up in my own feelings, I wasn't paying attention to the moment.

"Of course," Nik tells him, after a quick glance at me. His voice is perfect. Calm, deep, and soothing. He should do voice work. Though I'm pretty sure the camera would love him, too. How could it not?

When we step out of the office, we hear yelling. It takes us a minute to realize it's for us.

"Sean! Sean Reid!" We all turn to see where the voice is coming from. A woman and man dressed in polos and khaki slacks are approaching. The woman has a microphone while the man carries a big camera. Their faces seem familiar, but I can't immediately place them.

"Fuck," Mala whispers while smiling the world's biggest fake smile. Suddenly the reporters' names slam into my brain. They're the hosts of *Gretch & Clyde*, a nationally syndicated morning show.

Fuck is right. They're not quite a tabloid, but they are known for scoping out celebrity secrets. This can't be good.

"Fancy meeting you here," Gretchen says, sizing Sean up like a juicy steak.

"Lovely to see you, too, Gretchen," Sean counters. "Never tell me you're making an honest man out of Clyde."

She laughs politely, but it's clear that she knows something is up. Maybe she's just suspicious, maybe it's her reporter's instinct, but with Sean and Mala here, she smells a story. There's no way this won't make the news. Mala and Sean will be plastered all over the country's TV sets in moments.

"We're doing a weeklong feature on Vegas weddings," Clyde jumps in. "Featuring a different couple each night. Imagine how exciting it would be to have *you* as part of the story."

Gretchen's eyes gleam. "Think about it — 'the billionaire's Vegas bride.' I can see it now. The ratings will go through the roof!"

"Between you and the lovely Ms. Shah," says Clyde, "this will definitely go viral. We'll have to reach out to The Travel Network — I'm sure they'd be interested in the footage, too."

With every word Clyde and Gretchen speak, Sean's and Mala's expressions get more fixed. This could be disastrous for them both.

"I'm sorry to disappoint you," Nikhil jumps in, "but Sean and Mala aren't getting married. Cara and I are the lucky ones."

For a moment, everyone silently stares at each other.

Then Cara — she of the smooth skin and hazel eyes and generous mouth that I've been dreaming about for literal years — steps up.

"Sorry to disappoint you," she offers the reporters a sunny smile as she grabs my hand, "but it's just us regular, non-famous chickens."

"I'm sorry, I'm not familiar with —" She switches to that typical reporter voice. "Your names, please?"

"Dr. Nikhil Shah." I say automatically. Cara's grip is steady and warm. It's taking all my concentration for my brain to think about anything besides that.

"And you?"

"Cara Dunbar."

"You're one of the producers on FortyFab, aren't you?" Cara nods in reply, and Gretchen's eyes spark with interest. "How did you come to be here tonight?"

We exchange a glance. Cara gives me a besotted nod and a hand squeeze, as if to say *Go ahead, honey. Tell them.* Great.

"Just look at her." I wrap an arm around her waist. "I'd be the world's biggest fool not to lock this down."

Cara laughs and gives me a fond look, like I'm an idiot, but I'm *her* idiot, so it's all good.

"What I think Nik means to say," she tells them, "we've known one another for a long time, but saw each other again recently. This time, it was love at first sight. It's kind of a cliché, but we literally saw each other across a crowded room, and we just knew we belonged together."

I add in "But my job was difficult and dangerous. I didn't want to ask her to wait for me because of that — and who knew if that feeling between us would last? Now that I'm back, and have Cara by my side, I'm certain. We're meant to be together. It makes the time apart worth it."

Cara leans in and presses her lips to mine. Soft and quick, like she's done it a thousand times before and will do it a thousand times again. I barely have time to think *Holy shit, Cara Dunbar is kissing me* before it's over. That doesn't stop my heart from doing backflips in my chest.

"We're here because we just don't want to wait any more. We're ready to start the rest of our lives together."

"Well. Congratulations to you both." the woman says. I almost feel for her. She was hoping to break the internet with news about a tech billionaire getting hitched in Vegas. Instead, she's got a ramshackle story about two very non-famous people being a little bit extra about how much in love they are. If I were a betting man, and heard this cockamamie tale, I wouldn't give us a year.

"Let's take that picture now, love," I tell her. "Then we can go back in and get the license. She nods, then whips out her phone to take a smiling selfie of us outside of the office. We go back inside, and speak with the clerk. He steps away to grab forms for us.

"Holy shit," Cara mutters, keeping a smile on in case anyone is still watching. "That was quite the surprise."

"I'm impressed with your improv skils," I whisper back.

Continuing to play the doting soon-to-be husband, I grab her hands and rub them with my own. "Maybe you should be the one in front of the camera instead of Mala."

"Seeing as I'm the camera woman, that would be pretty difficult." She gives me a tiny smile and takes the forms from the clerk. Which makes me stare at her mouth. Which reminds me of that ever-so-delicate kiss. The gentle vanilla taste of her lips. If only we weren't in public. Then I could get this woman alone and kiss her the way she deserves to be kissed. I need —

What am I thinking? This isn't real. Our 'love' is something we literally made up five minutes ago to protect my cousin and her fiancé. I don't get to kiss this girl anymore. A flash of sadness washes over me at that thought.

I fill out my part of the forms, and pay the clerk. It takes a few minutes, but not long after we hand them over, Cara and I have got our marriage license. We pretend to look at it in awe, as if we really were getting married. Although I'm not quite sure I'm pretending.

Sean and Mala, playing along with us as the besotted couple, and them as our devoted friends, take pictures of us with the license, to keep up the facade.

We leave the office, and drive back to the hotel in silence. Sitting in the back of the limo, Cara reaches for my hand again. Who knows if the driver is a *Gretch & Clyde* fan? Happy for the excuse to touch her, I luxuriate in that simple contact. Her touch calms my jangly nervous system. I want — no, I need more of it. I am not an actor, and this is exhausting.

The hotel door — and freedom from this masquerade — is just a step away when I hear "Dr. Shah! Dr. Shah!"

It's that reporter again. She and her co-host must have followed us from the licensing office. They dash across the street to catch up to us.

"How can I help you?" I ask.

"You already have," she says, looking smug. "You're going viral. Just thought you should know."

"What are you talking about?"

She opens up a social media app that contains her video of Cara and me, giving our little spiel. It's been fifteen minutes at most, but it's already had tens of thousands of views. Even as we watch, the number continues climbing.

"Oh my gosh," Cara says. We exchange a look. "How on earth —?"

"We'd love to get your permission to film your actual wedding and maybe a day or two of your honeymoon—" The reporter continues to talk, although my brain refuses to process anything further. Viral means a very different something to me. I'm not sure how this changes things.

"We'll get back to you," Cara says firmly, and ushers us all into the hotel. The four of us head upstairs to Sean and Mala's suite.

Sean pours shots of Scotch for us all as the rest of us collapse onto the plush white sofas.

"Cara, Nik — oh my gosh. We are so sorry." Mala's face is a mask of distress. "We would never have asked you to offer yourselves up like that."

"We know you wouldn't ask," Cara tells her. "That's why we did it."

"What else would you expect from your bro/cousin, Mala?" She cheers up at my comment. If I can make light of it, it can't be that bad. Right?

Sean rubs his chin. "This is far above and beyond anything we'd ever ask. I'm grateful you wanted to protect us, but I'm not sure you two are ready for the scrutiny this will bring to your lives."

"We can handle a little scrutiny," I say, deliberately infusing confidence into my voice. "We just wait for it to pass. Surely an actual famous person will embarrass themselves within the next twenty four hours?"

"Sure," Mala offers, although she doesn't look super confident about her reply. "It's probably happening as we speak."

"In the meantime, we've got to get the two of you married."

Right. The whole reason we came to Vegas. In the hubbub over our newfound fame, I forgot that we never did make that wedding happen.

Sean and Mala had planned to visit one of the local chapels, but with reporters sniffing around and our temporary celebrity status, we agree that might not be such a great idea. A quick phone call to Cody is all it takes. While the four of us get cleaned up and change into more formal wear, he's arranged for a justice of the peace, flowers, and the wedding is back on.

Mala is radiant. I mean, my cousin is always beautiful (nope, not biased at all), but, cliché or not, she glows with happiness. And Sean — I've only known him for a little while, but until this moment, I had my doubts about his ability to smile. But for the entire ceremony, his face looks like the Chesire cat from Alice in Wonderland. He says "I do" like other people say yes to free guacamole.

I watch Cara's face, too. It's always been my favorite activity.

She has a quiet kind of beauty. The sort that sneaks up on you like an ocean wave. Those eyes that change from green to grey to brown in a moment could wreck a man on their shores. High cheekbones so sharp they could cut you, and a generous mouth I'm desperate to feel under my own again.

She's wearing her hair in a complicated pinned up way; all I want to do is take it down and run my fingers through those glorious curls. And her curves. She has all the curves. If I had to choose between getting my hands on her and my next breath, it would be a hell of a way to go.

In short, I didn't realize until this very moment that I have a type, but I do — and that type is absolutely, entirely, only Cara Dunbar.

The officiant pronounces Sean and Mala married. Cara and I

share a quick smile and look away as they kiss like it's going out of style.

I can't believe we managed it. Sean and Mala got married and no one is the wiser. They got to have their wedding their way. Helping them pull that off is worth any kind of trouble. Cara and I excuse ourselves to give them the privacy they deserve.

On the walk back towards our suite, we're both quiet, lost in our own thoughts. I pretend not to notice as Cara wipes away a tear, though I pass her a handkerchief. I'm a little choked up myself.

"That was nice." I say. I immediately want to kick myself. Nice. Could I be any more boring?

"It was perfect for them," she agrees. "Very intimate."

The look on her face is radiant. She's always been my cousin's best friend and cheering squad. The way Cara supports her friends is one of the things I admire most about her — and one of the reasons I never dared to make a move. From the start, I knew she and my cousins were friends for life, so if anything went wrong between us, there would be years of awkwardness to look forward to in my future.

But now. Now I'm thinking a little awkwardness might be worth the risk.

"Do you want to grab dinner?" I blurt out, before I lose my nerve.

She blinks at me, her changeable eyes so bright and vulnerable. Shoot. Maybe this is too far. Maybe my timing is off.

"Dinner. With you?" She questions. Like she can't quite believe I would ask.

"Unless you'd rather be alone?"

"No, no — I'm just in my head, a little." She rubs the back of her neck in an almost bashful way. A tiny smile curves her lip. "I'd love to have dinner with you."

"Great. Do you need a minute to change, or...?"

"No, I'm good. Let's just go."

I offer her my arm, and we get in the elevator.

"Do you mind if I check my messages real quick? My sister-in-law's due date is super close," she explains.

"Of course not." I pull out my phone and turn it back on so I can do the same.

I almost drop it when the flurry of messages comes through, buzzing one after the other. It feels like holding a beehive in my hand.

"Oh," Cara says. "Oh, no."

"What's that?"

"You know that video we were in?"

"Yeah?"

"It just passed five million views."

I make a strangled noise as she shows me the ticker on her phone. Once again, as we watch, the numbers go steadily upward.

Oh no, indeed. This can only mean one thing.

Here come the aunties.

For just a moment, Nikhil's face shows pure naked panic. I want to reach out, hold his hand, and tell him it's going to be okay. Before I can even try, he pulls himself together by sheer willpower.

"It'll be fine, Cara," he announces. I'm not sure which of us he's trying to convince: me or himself. "Although I am going to have to find an apology gift ASAP. My mother will not be happy."

I laugh. "I'm sure she'll understand, right? We were trying to do something nice for your cousin. That has to count in your favor."

Don't be too sure," he mutters, rubbing a hand across his face. "Mom loves me, and recognizes that I'm an adult, yeah, but she's been planning for my wedding since I was born. She'll have very strong opinions about this. I'm just grateful that she and my dad are visiting relatives in India right now."

Considering the freak out he seemed to be having a few minutes ago, I am a little shocked by the roguish grin that now crosses Nik's face. He puts his phone back on silent mode and tucks it back into his jacket pocket.

"But! Since they're already going to be furious with me," he shrugs, "I may as well leave that problem until tomorrow. You still up for that dinner?"

"... Okay?" I agree hesitantly. I want to have dinner with him, of course — I've wanted nothing more for ages — but the sudden about face is a little surprising.

"Compartmentalizing is a big part of saving lives in the field," he explains. "It also comes in handy in my personal life."

We leave the villas and head over to the restaurant. I wonder briefly if people will notice us. But no: even with all those viewers, the guests here at the resort will be focused on themselves and their own adventures.

Five million views. That's close to the numbers we get for FortyFab, the women's travel channel I started with my best friends. Thinking out our channel reminds me: Mala knows all about this, but our partner Siobhan is in Europe, visiting her family. I send her a quick text, but she's eight hours ahead. I won't hear from her for a while yet.

I look up to find Nikhil staring at me, an amused expression on his face. I bite my lip in embarrassment.

"Oh gosh, I'm so sorry." I tuck a wayward curl back in place. "I'm being rude."

Nikhil shakes his head. "It's fine. Gotta check in with your people, right? Any word on that new baby?"

"Nothing yet."

"Not to rain on your parade, but first babies tend to be late. You might have a long wait."

Oh, I hope not. My sister-in-law says she's ready to pop!"

Nik, as it turns out, has delivered something like a hundred babies in the course of his work. He probably knows what he's talking about. I decide not to share his stats with my brother's wife. It would only depress her.

We talk a little more on our walk. I'm struck again by how easy it is to talk to him. By how charming and warm he can be. I don't know why this secret side of him is out tonight, but I am reveling in it.

Before I know it, we're being shown into the restaurant. It's gorgeous, a modern rendition of a 1950s supper club. The entire place glows, from the marble fireplace and stone columns to the shimmering pillars and tureens filled with bottles of champagne. Even the brass tabletops are polished within an inch of their lives. Overstuffed chairs in clean neutrals and dusky deep green carpets ground the space and keep it from being a parody of excess. The effect is old-school, no holds barred elegance.

We're seated at a cozy table tucked behind a marble column and a plush green banquette. It's a perfect perch for seeing and not being seen. An internet-famous pair like ourselves won't be of any interest to the other patrons here. Looking around, I spot more than one actual celebrity at the tables around us. If anyone is looking for content, there are far juicier targets here.

I feel myself relaxing into this — meal? date? Whatever it is or isn't, my French 75 is making it even nicer. Nik chose the champagne-based cocktail, but I'm pretty sure it's my new favorite. I'm watching the bubbles gently pop when I hear Nikhil laugh under his breath.

"What's funny?"

"I — never mind." He looks a little embarrassed. "It's kind of dorky."

"Tell me," I demand. "I need something to take my mind off of this mess."

"Well, how do you feel about 80s hip hop?"

"My big brother David was more into that than me, but I know a little."

"Look at the end of the bar." He gestures over his shoulder. I scan down the row of gold and black barstools, looking for something out of place. I'm confused until I notice an enormous brass monkey.

I start humming the chorus to the old Beastie Boys song. Nikhil joins in, adding the trumpet noises for effect.

I shush him when the waiter approaches the table with appetizers, a strikingly plated dish with scallops, black truffles and chives. As soon as he walks away, Nikhil and I look at each other and start laughing again.

"Why? Of all the design choices..."

"I don't know," he says, wiping away a tear. "But I'm so glad you got that."

"Glad my inability to keep up with modern music finally came in handy."

"Same. If it wasn't made thirty years ago, I have no clue." He touches my hand briefly, a quick stroke meant to emphasize his point. My stomach leaps like I've got a ... what do you call a group of butterflies, anyway? Whatever it is, it's happening in there. I look down at my plate, hoping my feelings don't show on my face.

"Why the frown?" The concern in his voice drags my eyes up to his. "Is there's something wrong with your food?"

"No, no. My brain got stuck on something, and I can't resolve it, that's all."

"And I busted your chops for using your phone earlier." His eyes captivate me. Have they always been this luminous? Their deep brown color is as rich as the stone on the walls around us.

"Go ahead and look it up," he tells me. "I don't mind."

"No, really, it's fine," I reply. "With the show and everything, I'm always kinda... living in the future. Everything has to be prepared weeks or months in advance. I'm working on being more fully present these days. I'm taking a class from a friend of Mala's."

"That's difficult. Especially here." He gestures at the extravagant decor all around us. "This entire town is one enormous distraction."

"But it's also fun. That's worth something, too, right?"

It is." His expression turns serious. "Life's too short not to have fun when and where you can."

I hold up my drink. "We should toast. It's not official until we toast to it."

Nikhil clinks his glass with mine. "Well, then. Let's toast. To fun. And fake marriages."

I cover my face with my hand, which makes Nikhil laugh. I cannot believe we did that. Nor can I believe that we went viral for it. The internet is a wild and weird place.

"Oh, Dr. Shah..." I begin. Nikhil interrupts.

"No, my darling fake fiancée," he says to me, "Never Dr. Shah. You can only call me Nik. We've known each other for most of our lives *and* we're getting fake married."

"Thank you, Nik," I tell him, ignoring the thrill that spikes up my spine at the words *we* and *married* in the same sentence. "You're in the running for the top spot on my list of fake fiancés."

"In the running? Clearly I need to step it up."

"Relax. It's just a game."

"Doesn't matter," he says, staring into my eyes. "I always play to win."

There's a moment, then. He comes closer to me and I move closer to him, and our hands just barely touch. I am ninety-nine percent certain that he's about to kiss me. I am one hundred percent certain that it will be the hottest kiss of my entire life. The one that ruins me for all other kisses, all other men, for all time.

But then dinner arrives and we both back away from that cliff. Our conversation turns casual again. He's impressed that we're in talks with The Travel Network for a full half hour TV show. He also tells me more about the work he did with DWC. I can tell that he loved it, but being away from a close-knit family like his takes a heavy toll.

I admire it, but I don't think I could be away so much.

He points out how much travel we do for FortyFab, but I counter that it's not the same. I'm not put in dangerous situations like he is. I can't imagine flying into a war-torn country to be a healer when there's so much violence and desperation all around.

"I've never been the sort of person who runs toward the burning building," I say. "I'd only be in the way in an emergency."

"It's good to know your limits," he agrees. "But maybe worth pushing yourself out of your comfort zone?"

"Hmm," I say. I'll have to think on that more. "What draws you to it?"

"A sense of immortality I developed as a teenager, and never lost?" Half a smile sneaks across his face. "Truthfully, I feel like I have to, you know? Me being where I am, having the advantages I do? Just the luck of the draw. I feel the need to pay the universe back for that good luck."

Two hours fly by, and the next thing I know, we're closing down the restaurant. Nik offers me his arm as we leave; I happily take it.

We walk in silence, enjoying the cooler night air. I find myself stealing glances at him. Admiring his sharp cheekbones, the tumbling dark waves of his hair, his impossibly long lashes. Sigh.

I could get used to this.

"Hmm?" He looks down at me, solicitous as ever.

"What?"

"You sighed. Something on your mind?" He pays such close attention. It makes me a little nervous. But when someone is that attuned to you? It's also hot as fuck.

Of course, I think everything he does is hot. Him reading the phone book would be hot.

Do phone books even exist anymore? I need to look that up... which I won't be doing now, because I am being present and enjoying the moment. For real.

We've reached the steps of the villa. Nik takes a seat in the middle of the run.

"Talk to me," he demands, his long limbs stretched out in repose.

"I — it's just this situation." I blow a stray curl away from my face. "I know we're leaving it until tomorrow, but...I don't know. I go back and forth on whether we should ignore it or if we need to come up with a response."

"You were thinking all that on the walk over here?"

I duck my head, feeling heat in my cheeks. "I'm always thinking."

"Well, that has to stop." He pulls me toward him. The warmth of his hands on my shoulders takes my breath away. Nik doesn't seem to notice, though. He just scoots over and sits me on the step next to him, casually draping an arm around my shoulder.

"Look out there." He points toward the fairway, the gleaming green oasis laid out before us. It makes no sense in the desert, but it's striking nonetheless.

"What am I looking at?"

"All this shouldn't even be possible. But it's here. And for the rest of the week, we get to enjoy it. Rather than obsessing about a thing we can't deal with right now, because it's the middle of the night, I want you to look out there and really see."

I close my eyes, take in a deep breath. Hold it, then exhale. When I open them again, it's as if his words have boosted my vision. I can see the rolling slope of the greens, the creek that runs through the fairway, and the pines and palm trees beyond it. If I listen closely, I can hear the flow of water.

"It's beautiful," I admit. "Thank you for making me stop and appreciate it."

He leans into me, gives my shoulder a squeeze. "Very gracious of you to admit I'm right. This bodes well for our fake marriage."

"Not if you're going to gloat," I tease back. "That's very unsexy. Goes against your whole vibe."

His eyebrows skate up. "So you think I'm sexy? Interesting."

Oh shit. Did I really say that out loud?

"Obviously," I say, trying to turn it into a joke. "*My* fake fiancé has to be the sexiest, most charming, humblest — "

"There's not a man alive who could meet that standard, Cara."

He says my name so softly. Like it's as tender and delicate as this moment between us. "You'll have to settle for me."

I take his free hand in my own. "You are the farthest thing from settling."

He leans in, then, and grazes my lips with his own. The tenderest butterfly of a kiss, a gentle landing of his mouth on mine. Somewhere in there, my eyes closed. I stay there even after he pulls back. I can almost feel him looking at me.

"Did I break you?" He finally asks. I open my eyes, and climb into his lap. Settling myself against the rapidly growing proof of his interest, I give him a wicked grin.

"No, you didn't break me. But you're welcome to try."

He kisses me again, and it's so much better than I dreamed. Fierce and demanding, his kiss takes me apart, bit by bit, until I forget myself. All I can do is hold on to Nik as he plunders my mouth over and over, owning it, owning me, until I'm nothing but lust and need and want.

There's almost nothing that could stop me from giving in to this man, from letting him have his way with me. Even if he wanted to ravage me right here on these stairs, as long as he kept kissing me like this, I would absolutely allow it.

Unbelievably, the only thing that could stop me does. Dramatic throat clearing and a familiar-sounding voice steadily gets louder.

"Oh, my goodness. These two. So shameless. I can't believe they ran off without so much as a word to any of us —"

"Nik!" I pull up the strap of my dress, and try to quickly straighten my clothes. I'm sure my makeup is a mess, but there's only so much I can do without a mirror.

"Hmm? What is it?" He says, nibbling on my ear.

"Do you not hear that?" He cocks his head to the side. As the voices grow louder, he does a double take.

"Oh, shit." He grabs my hand and we run towards our door,

swiping the key card and making it inside in two minutes flat. We stand with our backs to the door and catch our breath.

"Maybe it wasn't them?" Nik offers. Before I can respond, the doorbell rings. We both jump guiltily.

"We know you're in there," they call. "Sean's assistant gave us your room number."

Sighing, I open the door. Outside are not only Nik's uncle and aunt, but the two people I most love — and least want to see right now.

"Hi, Mom. Hi, Dad."

Nik

It's funny: I've been in a lot of dicey situations in my career. Flying into countries where danger was all around, trying to help civilians caught in the middle of two groups that were fighting — I thought I'd seen it all and nothing could phase me.

That is, until I find myself greeting my fake fiancée's parents at the door of our suite with a raging hard on.

I'm shuffling my jacket from arm to arm, trying to cover my crotch while also being respectful of the Dunbars, as well as my Auntie Meena and Uncle Ravi.

Mrs. Dunbar comes over to us first. She offers me a smile and a tender hug that I absolutely don't deserve. Lynn has always been the most elegant woman I know. Cara's beautiful brown complexion, head full of curls and gentle heart come from her.

"Nikhil," she says, surprised. "I thought you were in Bangladesh."

The Dunbars have lived next door to Auntie and Uncle since forever, so I'm not surprised that Lynn is mostly up-to-date on my work life. My family never misses a chance to brag on me.

"My leave coincided with Aesha and Theo's big party, and I wanted to be here for the wedding, so it made sense to come back."

"It's good to see you." Mr. Dunbar shakes my hand with a little more firmness than is strictly necessary. Mike's an older white dude, with bright blue eyes and hair that's more salt than pepper. Every time I see him, I think he'd make a great Santa Claus. "Although the circumstances are a little strange."

Strange is an extremely polite way of putting it. I run a hand through my hair, knowing I'm disheveled from the intense make-out session they interrupted.

Cara, of course, looks perfect. Sure, her curls are a little messy from me running my hands through them, and her lipstick is all worn away, but she still looks absolutely amazing. Maybe that's cocktail goggles, but I don't think so. The moment we kissed on those steps, I felt sober as a judge. Even now, every part of my body still feels a little zing at the memory of her nearness.

My aunt pinches my arm.

"Ow! Auntie! What was that for?"

"Because your uncle asked you a question, and you didn't respond. You're just mooning over Cara."

"When did this happen, beta?" Uncle chimes in. "You never even told us you two were dating and now you're running off to get married?"

"Which we found out from the television." Mrs. Dunbar adds. "Honey, your cousins and friends were texting and calling me to ask about this. Even your grandmother heard."

Shit. Cara and I exchange a look. Her guilty conscience is all over her face; I'm sure mine is too. Neither of us thought about the ramifications for the rest of our families. We dove into this fake arrangement on a whim, never suspecting that we would have to face the music in the real world.

"Mom, Dad," Cara begins, "I'm — we're both so sorry. We would never have wanted to upset you. Any of you. The truth is —"

"We panicked," I jump in. I deliberately avoid Cara's gaze. "Neither of us is used to having reporters get in our faces and ask us questions. They thought Sean and Mala were getting married, so they were making a big production of it…"

"Ach, so obnoxious. As if my daughter would get married in secret." Auntie's face is a study in disgust. "Mala knows better."

Cara squeezes my hand. No doubt she's biting her tongue as hard as I am.

"But now, you two are allegedly engaged," Cara's dad pipes up. "Is this for real, or were you just trying to stop them from bothering Mala and Sean?"

We could not ask for a more perfect opening. Mike lined it up, and all we have to do is take the shot.

So why isn't Cara speaking up? Why aren't I? We just look at each other, staring a little too long. My uncle makes a face and puts us out of our misery.

"Come on, Mike. I'd expect Nikhil to do something crazy like that, but Cara? No way. She's always been a good girl. If she's involved, then it's real."

"I'm thirty-nine years old, for heaven's sake," Cara mumbles. There's not any heat in it, though. She knows the deal. No matter how old we get, they will always see us as children.

"You're not the one he's calling a lunatic, though, are you?" I whisper back. She makes a weird little snorty sound. Even under these circumstances, it is adorable.

Lynn clears her throat. "Cara, can I speak to you privately, please?"

"Is that necessary, Mother? There's nothing you can say to me that my fiancé shouldn't hear." I bite my tongue to keep from laughing. I guess it's true that being around our parents makes us act like bratty teenagers again. She's really playing this up.

"Sweetheart, I don't want to be rude or… indelicate…" Lynn's voice trails off. Cara and she do some kind of weird back-and-forth contest of wills that ends in an exasperated sigh and an eye roll.

"You can relax, parents," she announces. "This isn't because I'm pregnant."

I'm startled, but I watch everyone's faces after she makes the announcement. Pretty sure Mike and Uncle Ravi would die before admitting it, but they look relieved.

"This is so sudden, honey," Mike throws in. "We did wonder."

"I never thought that, sweet girl," Aunt Meena tells her, patting Cara's hand. "I told them all on the plane that you had too much sense to get married because of that."

Oh, my god. My family actually discussed my sex life. With other people. They actively contemplated whether or not I had so much sex with Cara that I knocked her up. I mean, it only takes one time, but still. I might die of embarrassment. Why is there never a sinkhole when you need one?

"But," Auntie continues. "This is all over the Internet now. We need to get control of this before it gets any more out of hand."

She scans our hands. "You didn't do the ceremony part, no?"

"No," I say. "I haven't even gotten her a proper ring yet."

My aunt makes an annoyed noise. It's basically, *Ugh, men.* I give her a sheepish grin. She ruffles my hair, which has now decided to flop into my face in the most annoying way. I know I look like my teenaged self, a kid with more hair than sense. Which is how she still thinks of me, so I guess that fits.

"Thank goodness for you two that we're here, then," she tells me. "We'll have everything together for a ceremony on Friday."

"Sorry, say that again?" I'm sure I heard her wrong.

"We can't let you do this all willy nilly," Lynn replies. "Meena and I are putting everything together. It will be perfect. Your cousins and grandparents are already on their way."

"Now, you two run off to your room and get settled in. We have a lot to do and not much time. Early start tomorrow, eh?"

Mike and Uncle Ravi grab the luggage. "Which rooms should we put these in?"

"Um..."

"Never mind, we'll find them."

Oh, crap. We can't let them see that until about fifteen minutes ago, Cara and I were definitely sleeping in separate beds.

"Dad, why don't you and Mr. Shah grab a drink?" Cara offers. She's clearly thinking the same thing. "They have that Glenlivet you both like on the bar. Nik and I will deal with the bags."

"There's a great view of the golf course from the balcony," I add. That seems to seal the deal. Mike and Uncle Ravi are happy to relax while Cara and I load up their luggage and hustle over to my former room in a daze. We quickly rearrange everyone's belongings, settling her parents' things in one room, and my aunt and uncle in the bedroom across the hall, and dragging my bags to the other side of the apartment. Lynn and Auntie are so busy they don't even notice us.

When we're done, Cara flops down on the bed. The very large, one and only bed in this room. Which we will both be sleeping in. Gingerly, I sit beside her.

"We are so screwed."

"And not in the good way," I mumble. She laughs. The sound loosens the knot in my chest.

"What on earth are we going to do, Nik?"

"Right now? We're gonna go to sleep, and figure things out in the morning."

Cara looks at me and shrugs. "You keep reminding me. But you're right: there's nothing we can do tonight except stress out. I think we've done enough of that already.

"Mind if I hop in the shower first?" I shake my head.

Cara quickly rummages around, grabbing a few things from the room's dresser and closet before heading into the massive bath.

I unpack my own luggage while she's in the bathroom. I take my time making room for my clothes and finding the sweats I sleep in, since I am very specifically not imagining her in the shower. I don't think of the soft blonde curls that she probably pinned up, leaving her swanlike neck exposed. I don't imagine her light brown skin, glistening from the water pouring down from the shower head, or the slow, deliberate way she's probably washing her body, covering every inch of her in smooth suds —

"All yours!" Cara steps out of the bathroom. Her face is dewy and slightly flushed; I guess that's the result of all those fancy bottles on the counter. She's braided her hair in a long fishtail that hangs in the middle of her back, and she's wearing a silky-looking dark red pajama top and matching shorts. I blink, confused at the transition from the sexy siren in my fevered imagination to the way she looks in real life.

Bare faced, pajama-wearing Cara is... cute. Still sexy, still hot, but also really, really cute.

"Nik?" She gently rubs my shoulder. "You okay?"

"Yeah, yeah," I say, realizing that staring at her and drooling is not a good look. "Sorry, just..."

She gives me a warm smile. "All good. It's been a long day. See you in a bit."

I grab that pair of sweats and head into the bathroom. The space is already steamy from Cara's shower. I strip off my things and get under the water, hoping the heat and steam will relax me.

We can do this. We're adults. It's not a big deal, us sharing a bed. We've done it before.

I laugh at myself. Camping on the floor of Auntie and Uncle's basement at ages nine and eleven hardly counts as sharing a bed.

And adult me sleeping next to curvy, sexy, grown-up Cara in this bed is a very different prospect.

Especially after that make-out session on the stairs.

I groan at the memory of her in that dress. Kissing her, touching her, sliding those little straps down her shoulders.... Fuck. At this rate I'll be hard as a rock all night.

I can't make her uncomfortable or assume that she wants to pick up where we left off.

I'll just — relieve myself. Then we can both get some sleep and figure out how to manage our families in the morning.

Almost as soon as I have the thought, my dick responds. My

favorite memory flashes in my mind. Cara at my cousin's engagement party. Even behind that mask, I knew who she was immediately. Those gorgeous hazel eyes gave her away.

Of course, that one shoulder dress she wore didn't hurt either. A rich, warm shade of pink, it clung to her curves, pushing her breasts up like an offering. I wanted to take a bite.

I dreamed about her in that dress. About sliding the zipper down just enough to peel the bodice away from her tits. I'd stroke her rosy brown nipples, make her gasp with pleasure. She'd sink down to her knees, dress billowing around her, and unfasten my clothes, desperate to get at my cock.

She'd stroke me just right, running her nails along my length, until I was hard as granite. Then I'd push her tits together and slide my cock in between them, feeling her hot breath over the tip just before she dips her head down for a lick —

A slight noise jerks me out of my filthy fantasy. My eyes fly open. Instead of imaginary Cara, all dressed up and hungry for me to make her dirty, I see the real her standing in the bathroom doorway. Watching me beat off while fantasizing about her.

Oh, fuck.

Cara

Oh, fuck.

I'm so busted.

I didn't mean to perv on him. After my shower, I tried to settle down for the night. To ignore the fact that Nikhil Shah and I were about to share the same bed. The thing I've dreamt about since puberty —although my ideas of what might happen in that bed have gone from PG to XXX as I grew up.

I'd tried to read, but couldn't focus.

Maybe it was too warm. I took off my pajama top, leaving the stretchy ribbed tank underneath. Or maybe it was the sound of running water that distracted me. Making me imagine Nik standing under the water, tiny little rivers streaming over his shoulders, sliding down his pecs and abs and thighs and holy fuck, I was so horny I could not even think.

When I looked up from my book, I realized two things: one, that the bathroom door was wide open and two, those shower doors are crystal clear glass — they'd leave nothing to the imagination.

I got up to close the door. When I walked over to the bathroom, though, I froze. Because there, behind that glass, Nik was entirely naked.

The sight of him was even better than I imagined — and I'd imagined this a lot. Glistening brown skin, swooping dark hair, and an ass so tight you could bounce a quarter off it: the man is pretty fucking perfect. I think I stopped breathing for a few seconds.

Then I watched him soap and scrub and rinse his back. Honestly, I never thought I wanted to to be a washcloth before, but perhaps that was hasty of me. I should really reconsider.

Oh, God. How am I such a pervy mess? I scolded myself. *I'm closing this door and I'm walking away.*

And I absolutely meant it.

But then he turned around and I got to see him in all his glory.

There was a lot to be seen.

My pussy clenched at the sight of his cock, long and thick and rigid. I imagined how he would feel, filling me, stretching me, thrusting into me over and over — the very thought had me desperately clenching my thighs together.

For a moment, he rested his head against the tile.

"Fuck, fuck, fuck." He whispered. "Fuck, Cara."

Shit. A spear of anxiety twisted through my guts. Had he seen me? Oh, God. There's nothing I can say to excuse this —

"How am I gonna sleep next to you like this?"

Nik breathed heavily for a moment. Then he straightened up, like he'd come to a decision.

He lathered up his hand and started to stroke his cock. He took his time about it, using smooth, slow gliding motions. The pace seemed like torture but made him grunt a little under his breath. My pussy throbbed in time with the movements of his hand.

I should walk away.

I should join him.

What would he do if I did?

How would calm, controlled Nik react if I threw my clothes on the floor and slipped into the shower with him? It's big enough for two.

Would he let me run my hands all over his slick skin, grazing his taut muscles with my fingernails? Would he let me help, wrapping his hand over mine and showing me how tight he likes the grip? Would we stroke his cock together, faster and faster until he comes, shuddering and gasping for breath?

My breasts are heavy, diamond hard nipples straining against the fabric of my tank top.

I glide a hand across them, sliding down, down into my pajama shorts. Still watching Nik's movements, I press firmly against my clit, desperate to relieve the pressure building up in me.

I match him stroke for stroke, sliding two fingers up and down, up and down. Close my eyes. Wish it was his hand instead of my own. The thought wrings a whimper from my throat.

It's just a tiny noise, but it's enough. Nik's eyes zoom open and he freezes mid-stroke. I just freeze.

"Cara." He whispers my name on a breath. Then he looks at me — really looks at me. He sees how tight my nipples are, against the thin fabric of this tank top, and where my hand is, and he gets a look I've never seen on his face before.

I start to pull my hand away.

"Don't." He calls out, and I instantly hold still.

Nik turns off the water and gets out of the shower. Dripping wet, without a stitch on, he strides over to the bathroom doorway.

When he reaches me, he stares down at me for a moment. Like he's deciding what to do with me. I lick my lips, and his brown eyes darken with something possessive as they follow my tongue.

Before I can even think of anything to say Nik reaches out, gently but firmly gripping the back of my neck and pulling me into him. Then his mouth comes down on mine.

This kiss is different than the one on the steps. I'd thought that was intense. Now, he's even bolder, kissing me so long and so deep that I can't breathe. Every other sensation — the solid weight of his body pressing me against the door, the warmth of his damp skin, the friction of my very thin top between his pecs and my breasts — is second to the dangerous, demanding way he takes my mouth.

He owns me, and all we've done is kiss.

Nik pulls away from my lips, dipping his head down to my neck. I half gasp, half giggle when he nuzzles that one spot right behind my ear. He laughs in return, mouth still pressed against my skin, and it sends a jolt of electricity down my spine.

"Cara." Ugh, even the way he says my name turns me on. "I need to see you."

"Wha — mmm?" He sucks one nipple through the fabric of my tank, scattering my thoughts and making my clit ache.

"Take these off and show me what you were doing."

My body flushes, simultaneously embarrassed and turned on. "Oh, God — Nik —"

"Here," he says. "Let me help you."

He shoves the shorts off of my body, leaving me in nothing but my tank top. It's warm in here, but I can't help shuddering at how exposed I am. No one else has seen me like this.

He lifts me onto the counter. I make a startled noise as the cool marble touches my bare skin. Nik kneels in front of me, like he's offering a prayer at an altar, and I am about to be the sacrifice.

"Let me see you, beautiful girl," he orders again, spreading my legs apart. God, it's too much. I close my eyes. Him looking at the most intimate part of me with heat in his gaze is too much.

Nik takes my hand. Pries opens my tightly clenched fists. Kisses my palm. Delicately, he takes two of my fingers in his hand, gliding them over my slick folds. I try to hold back a moan, but I can't resist.

"You lovely, dirty girl," he murmurs, planting a kiss on the inside of my knee. "Is this what you did while you watched me? You touched yourself like this?"

He swirls my fingers in an infinite loop around my clit, going faster now. I'm completely drenched, and the sounds of our fingers sliding through my wetness is utterly lewd.

"Y -- yes," I gasp.

"Did you know I was thinking of you the entire time?" he demands. His tone is mild, but his eyes are fierce and dark as they stare into my own. "That I wished it was you with every stroke of my hand?"

He takes my other hand, slides two fingers inside me. I cry out in shock and pleasure. He slowly pumps them in and out.

"I wanted it to be you, Cara," he continues. murmuring into my skin. Steadily thrusting with those fingers. "I wanted your hand. Your mouth. Your pussy. Didn't matter. Just as long as some part of you was wrapped around my cock."

Fuck. I might die. Is it possible to die of too many dirty, sexy words whispered into your flesh? I'm close to it. I'm so, so close.

At the first swipe of his tongue, I cry out. My hips buck, trying to scoot away from the overload of sensation. Nik pins me in place with a firm hand. His other one keeps up that piston-like slide, in and out, in and out. He's relentless, flicking and sucking and twisting, and it doesn't take long before I break. I come so hard it almost hurts, sobbing, gasping, shattering in a million pieces, all over his hands and tongue.

Nik reaches behind me, fumbling in a basket atop the sink. I catch my breath while he sheaths himself with the condom. He slides into me, smooth and deep and perfect. Frantic, I pull him closer. Kiss him deeply. Taste myself on his tongue. I can't get enough. I'll never get enough of this man.

He fucks me hard and steady even as he keeps up a stream of dirty talk. "You're so fucking perfect." "You take my cock so good." His words make my hips rise to meet his. To fuck him back just as good. I'll be his beautiful, perfect girl who takes his cock if that's what he needs.

Nik's rhythm speeds up, then turns erratic. His whole body

shudders, and his eyes close as his orgasm hits. I've never seen anything hotter than Nikhil Shah coming inside me. I already know I never will again.

He kisses me on the forehead, before sliding out of me and dealing with the condom. By mutual consent, we get back into the shower — together this time. Although strictly speaking, there's more kissing and touching than actual showering. Our attempt at efficiency ends with me bracing my hands on the built in seat and Nik balls deep inside me yet again.

We just barely manage to moisturize ourselves before collapsing into the bed, limbs tangled together, sleep hitting us like a wave.

"What does this mean, Nik?"

"Wait til morning, love. We'll figure it out in the morning."

"Don't say love unless you mean it," I mutter.

I'm almost asleep when he whispers back.

"How do you know I don't?"

In the morning, I wake up with a mouthful of hair.

At some point during the night, Cara's nightcap/scarf thingy must have slipped off of her curls, because the end of her braid is somehow both halfway up my nose and halfway down my throat.

Okay. Slight exaggeration. The little fishtail is tickling my lips, and I can smell whatever that fruity flowery product is that she rubs into her hair. I press her braid to my face and inhale deeply.

"You know I can feel that, right?" she asks on a laugh. Cara turns over, her long legs tangling with mine.

"I can't help it. You smell delicious." I roll over on top of her. The softness of her body underneath me is intoxicating. "Good enough to eat."

I dip my head down for a kiss, but she shrieks and wiggles out from under me.

"Oh, no," she says, still laughing. "I don't know exactly what we're doing here, Nik, but what we're not gonna do is inflict morning breath on each other."

She whisks the sheet off of the bed and dashes off to the bathroom. I stare after her, just barely catching myself before I let out a wistful sigh. I've got it bad for this woman and I'm too far gone to even be embarrassed.

That doesn't mean I know what to do about this whole situation, however. It was one thing when random strangers on the internet were curious; I figured that would blow over quickly. Now that our families are involved — and now that our relationship has changed — it's a whole different ballgame. Lucky for me, my parents are in Punjab visiting relatives. At least they're not around to see the mess I've created with my impulsive scheme.

I turn on my phone and leave it on the bed while I get dressed. This time I'm prepared for the onslaught of messages, so even when the buzz of incoming texts goes on for ages, I ignore it. Cara and I trade places, so I can do my morning routine while she dresses.

I shamelessly ogle her while she slips into a bright blue summer dress and lightweight cardigan. When she adds a pair of sandals with straps that wrap all the way up to her thighs, I have to fight the urge to drag her back to bed.

While I'm talking my inner caveman down, Cara comes back into the bathroom. She rubs a bit of oil on her hands while she takes down her braid, letting her loose blonde curls billow out across her shoulders. I can't resist twirling one around my fingers, pulling it out like a spring.

"Knock it off, Nik," she mock grumbles. She takes the curl firmly out of my reach and twists her hair up into a puffy ponytail. I lean down and nuzzle her neck while she does so.

"Would you stop?" She asks playfully, turning around in my arms. I take that kiss she denied me earlier. By the time we break apart, the wild look in her eyes proves I'm not the only one thinking of going back to bed.

"Do you really want me to stop?"

Cara hesitates before she speaks. "Nik, we really should talk."

"I know." I slide a hand up and down the curve of her hip. She leans into the touch. My other hand draws a spiral on her collarbone. She makes a contented noise.

"We need a plan."

"Yep." I kiss along the curve of her jaw. Her head falls back onto my shoulder.

"Something other than sex, Nik."

"Tell me you don't want that," I demand. Before she can answer, I capture her mouth again, the taste of mint and citrus still fresh on her lips.

Her body melts into mine, soft and lush. I slide my hands underneath the hem of her dress. She moans as I glide them over her hips, her round ass, the perfect little dip of her waist. By the time I make my way up to her breasts and undo her bra, my dick is rock hard.

I maneuver us over to the bed, laying her on her back. With her kiss-swollen lips, hooded eyes, and dress hiked up above her exposed tits, she looks debauched. Like all of my fantasies come to life.

I bend down, taking one plump nipple in my mouth, teasing the other into a peak with my fingertips.

"Oh, damn, Nik," Cara moans. She threads her fingers through my hair with one hand while the other works at my belt. When she gets her hands on my cock and starts to stroke and squeeze, I can't hold back a curse. It feels too good.

I need this. I need her.

I switch my attentions to the other breast, swirling my tongue around the tip, giving it just the tiniest bite. The way she gasps and tightens her grip on my cock let me know she approves.

I've got my fingers hooked in the waistband of her underwear when the sexy little noises she's making turn into startled ones.

"Wait, Nik, hold on," she says, reaching beneath her and pulling out my phone. The distinctive sound of my mother's favorite song cools me off faster than a cold shower. Shit. Reluctantly, I roll away and answer the call. Cara grabs her bra and heads into the bathroom to give me privacy.

"Hi Mata-ji—"

"Nikhil Ishan Shah, have you lost your mind?"

"Mom—" I tuck the phone under my ear so I can rearrange my clothes. "It's not like that—"

"You know Daddy and I weren't coming home until next month. Now I hear from the internet that you're getting married?" She makes a disgusted noise. My stomach plunges into my shoes. This just keeps spiraling out of control.

"It was a spur of the moment decision —"

"Well your spur of the moment is pricking Daddy and me in the bum, beta. We have to rearrange our entire trip."

"No, Mom, don't do that—"

"And miss my son's wedding? Cha. We'll work it out. I'm just glad Meena and Ravi are there. I'll text you both when our plans are set."

"Mom, really —"

"I have to go. Love you, reckless boy." I try to protest, but she's already gone.

Hey." Cara gently bumps my shoulder. She's all put together again. I both admire and regret her efficiency.

"You okay?"

"Yeah," I confirm, running a hand through my hair. "You know how my parents are. Mom in particular. She's a whirlwind."

"They adore you, you know." She's right, and normally, I'm grateful. But sometimes, I could really do with a little less love and a lot more chill.

I stand up and stretch. Time to face the gauntlet. I hold out my hand; Cara takes it. Her palm is cool in mine. We still don't have a plan, but at least we're in this together.

The living room of the suite has been transformed. The table is covered in lists and brochures and fabric samples, and Aunt Meena and Mrs. Dunbar are deep in conversation with Cody, the butler.

"Good morning, darlings." Mrs. Dunbar sings. "There's food and coffee on the bar. We ordered in since we weren't sure when you'd be awake."

"Thank you," I say. We drift over to that side of the room and load up plates. After all our exertions last night, we're both famished.

Sean and Mala arrive while we're having breakfast. By the level of enthusiasm in their greetings, you'd think it had been years instead of hours since we last saw each other. It's hard to believe so much has changed in twenty-four hours.

Between them, they keep the elders occupied while Cara and I scarf down our food. Even better, they convince Aunt Meena and Mrs. Dunbar to let us escape with them. We dash out the door before they can change their minds.

As soon as we get away from the villa, Sean turns to us.

"Sorry they ambushed you. Mala's parents are our emergency contacts. I guess they convinced my assistant that your impending nuptials were an emergency."

"Having their attention on us means we kept your secret out of the news," Cara adds. "That's something."

Mala sighs. "But now *my* mother is here, *your* mother's here, and my aunt and uncle are driving themselves crazy figuring out how to get from Punjab to Vegas in time for the ceremony."

"Let me handle that, lass?" Sean says. "We can get them on a private plane there and back in no time."

"I guess this is one of those problems we can throw money at," she concedes, smiling up at her partner — no, I catch myself. He's her husband now.

"Are we sure it's even necessary to bring them here?" Cara interjects. "This is an awful lot of effort considering Nik and I aren't — I mean, we should think about this. Isn't going to all this trouble kind of insane?"

Mala and Sean shrug. "Sean and I are willing to come clean about getting married. It might look somewhat shady at first, but ultimately, we could pull it off. The public will be sympathetic to us wanting privacy."

"Auntie and Uncle will lose their shit, Mala," I point out. "They're already beside themselves over didi's wedding. This will make them nuts."

"I'll take responsibility," Sean assures us. "I'm still in good graces, being new to the family. Besides, we'll let Meena plan whatever kind of celebration she wants. That'll go a long way towards smoothing this over."

I look over at Cara, who is frowning into her phone. She swears under her breath.

"What is it, hon?" Mala asks.

"There's a post here from Doctors Who Care." Cara pushes back a stray curl before going on. "They've reposted the story from Gretchen & Clyde's show. With a thank you for the crazy increase in donations."

She hands me her phone. My eyes pop at the numbers. It's money my ex-employer desperately needs to continue helping people in the toughest areas in the world.

Cara and I look at each other, and at Mala and Sean. Her expression is calm, but her beautiful hazel eyes flash with the panic she's trying to hide.

"Well, then," Cara announces. There's a grim finality in her voice. "I guess we really do have to get married."

The four of us are silent, contemplating our new reality.

"If it's a question of money —" Sean starts.

I hold up a hand to stop him. "It's not just the money, Sean — and you've already been extremely generous with DWC. It's more about potential damage to their reputation."

"If we come out and say we lied," Cara adds, "that we weren't really together, people would claw back their donations — maybe not everyone, but a lot of people. DWC would take a hit because they're associated with us."

Sean looks at Mala for confirmation. She frowns.

"Hate to say it, but I agree. There's an enormous risk here."

"I'm sorry," he says again, shaking his head in disgust. "This falls squarely on my head."

"Not at all, Sean." Cara tells him. "This is on those nosey reporters who don't know how to respect people's privacy."

"So, listen," Mala declares, sounding exactly like Aunt Meena, "we have wedding chores to handle. Sean and I can do some of these ourselves, but there is one thing you two might want to do on your own..." She wiggles her hand purposefully.

"Right! The ring." My heart does a weird little patter. I have to go buy wedding rings. With my fake fiancée. Who's not so fake any more.

The four of us part ways with a quick round of hugs. Sean pulls me aside.

"Listen," he whispers to me, "I don't know how to make this less awkward —"

"Sean," I tell him, "if you offer me money to buy this ring, I swear, I'll kick you in the balls."

"Understood," he laughs, giving me a mock salute. Despite my threat, I appreciate his attempt to be supportive. It's not his fault he's still new at helping without instantly offering cash. That's what most people want from him. But he'll learn.

"It has to be at least a year, don't you think?" Cara asks. We walk hand in hand into the resort's retail complex. There's a mix of brands I know — Cartier, Balmain, Saint Laurent — and more exclusive ones I've never heard of. I can't help contrasting this moment with my time in Belgium or Uzbekistan. There was no thought of luxury then.

"Our marriage?" I shrug. "Sure." A year gives us time. Time enough for people to forget about our brief moment of internet fame, and for all those donations to DWC to stick.

And maybe, just maybe, time enough for something more to develop between us.

Cara pulls me toward a jewelry store on the right side of the arcade. When we enter, the young lady behind the counter gives us a very professional smile and greeting until she gets a good look at us.

"Oh, my gosh. You're the *Gretchen & Clyde* couple!" she squeals. "In my store! I shouldn't ask, but: can we please take a selfie?"

I look at Cara, who shrugs. We take the picture and start to explain what we need when a too-familiar voice interrupts.

"Well, good morning! If it isn't our viral lovebirds." We turn to see Gretchen and Clyde and their enormous video camera. The saleswoman blushes guiltily.

Beside me, Cara's body language changes: shoulders back, chin up, smile in place. I hate that she's got to fake it, but I love that she's so willing to support Doctors Who Care.

"You haven't tied the knot yet?" Clyde asks. Both he and Gretchen have that hearty TV reporter speak down pat. I wonder if they talk to each other that way when the cameras are off.

"Good morning," Cara replies. "No, we haven't yet, and that's thanks to you two."

Gretchen's eyes light up. "Is that right? Do tell."

Cara gives them a short version of our story, while I try to look encouraging and throw in the occasional comment. My not-so-fake fiancée is a rock star.

"That's wonderful," Gretchen says. "So now you're doing it the traditional way — sort of. Just on a tighter timeline. This will be a very brief engagement indeed."

"Man to man, Dr. Shah," Clyde interjects, "I'm not great with jewelry. I'm curious: have you two talked about the ring? Do you know your fiancée's taste well enough to choose it on your own?"

What the hell, Clyde? Why is he testing me? It's all about the ratings with these two, I know, but this is my life. Even if our engagement is only going to last a couple of days, I'm taking it seriously. Eff that guy.

Cara, sweetheart that she is, looks up at me adoringly. "We

haven't really discussed it, but Nik has wonderful taste. I'm sure he'll choose something perfect."

"You sure, love?" I put an arm around her. Even though we're being filmed, it's feels so damned good to touch her.

"Of course," she tells me, eyes glowing. "I trust you."

We figure out her size, and then Cara steps away while the saleswoman shows me the ring selection. There are dozens of them. My brain glazes over at the plethora of shiny baubles. So many cuts and metals and colors of stone. A surprising number of the diamonds look big enough to poke your eye out.

But when I see the one, I know.

It has a square, bright green gemstone surrounded by gold, with tiny diamonds all around the edge. The matching band features those same tiny diamonds halfway around the band as well.

"This one," I declare. "This is it. What do you think, hon?"

Cara comes over to look at my selection. When she gasps, I know I've gotten it right.

"Nik, Wow." That sweet, vulnerable look is on her face again. "It's gorgeous."

"Let's see how it feels." I slip the ring onto her left hand.

"It's perfect," she says. Her eyes are bright with tears. Before I know it, she's kissing me, so sweet and perfect. I never want it to end.

Clyde clears his throat with more drama than is strictly necessary. Cara and I break apart, laughing. I want to go back for more, video be damned.

"Show us the ring, would you, Ms. Dunbar?" Gretchen asks. "I'm sure the viewers would love to see it."

"Dr. Shah, tell us why you chose it," Clyde adds.

I don't want to say. It's personal. But if it'll make them go away and let me get back to kissing Cara, so be it.

"The stone caught my eye first. It's green, but also has a warm brown tone to it. Like Cara's eyes."

The saleswoman throws in "It's a princess cut peridot. They have that effect."

"Then I looked at the color and shape. It's gold, which looks beautiful next to her skin, and the profile of it is low. Cara's got a very physical job. She's always carrying around equipment, setting up shots for the show she works on, so I wanted to pick something that was less likely to get caught up in a cable, or whatever."

Clerk again: "It's a bezel setting, with a halo of pavé diamonds around the gemstone."

"Finally, the style feels old-fashioned style to it, and she loves that kind of thing. So it's beautiful, yet practical. Just like Cara."

"Whew," Gretchen fans herself. "For a man of science, you certainly know how to speak to the heart, Dr. Shah. I know our viewers at home are swooning as much as I am right now."

Clyde agrees. "To the guys out there, I hope you're paying close attention. This is how it's done."

Mercifully, they stop taping the two of us. Clyde and Gretchen take some more shots of the store, and chat more with the clerk. Cara and I park ourselves in a corner of the store, out of camera sight, and wait for them to finish.

I watch her out of the corner of my eye, wanting her reaction now that the spotlight isn't on us. She watches the taping — professional interest, I suppose — but every so often, stares down at the ring on her hand with this tiny little smile. I'm so proud I could burst.

When the filming ends, we settle the bill and rejoin the family. The rest of the day goes by in a blur — picking a cake, finding a suit for me, a dress for Cara, and coordinating outfits for the bridesmaids and groomsmen. Not to mention meals with our folks, confirming my parents' travel, and an endless sea of texts from all the relatives and friends who are traveling to join us here.

By ten o'clock, we're back in our suite. Although we're exhausted, when she reaches out for me, I reach back.

Our lovemaking is different this time. Slower. Sweeter. Deeper.

I don't care if our relationship started under false pretenses. This feels true to me. There's no reason she can't grow to love me the way I —

The way I love her.

I'm in love with Cara Dunbar.

It's not just the sex. It's her. Her dedication to FortyFab. The way she wrinkles her nose when she's trying not to laugh. That giggle when I kiss the ticklish spot behind her ear. The way she looks at me when we're alone, with this sweet, open expression that makes me want to grab her and never let go.

Afterward, we lie together. She's naked, golden brown skin and magnificent curves tempting me even now that we're sated. I can't seem to stop touching her. She leans into my touch like a cat.

"Hey," she says, expression serious. "About the ring."

"Hmm?" I'm half asleep. "You really do like it, right?"

"I love it. It's perfect." She raises up on her elbows, giving me a perfect view of her tits that makes me wish I weren't so tired.

"I want to pay for half of it."

"What? Absolutely not."

"Nik, be sensible." She looks confused at my reluctance. "It's not like we're getting married for the usual reasons. It shouldn't cost you this much, too."

"No. Leave it alone." I know my tone is harsh, but I can't help it. Her words are like a sock in the face. But she's right. We aren't getting married because we're in love.

At least she isn't.

"But Nik —"

"I'm done with this. I'm not taking your money. Final answer." I turn over, ending the conversation, feigning sleep.

Although I lie there for a long time, wondering how on earth I got this so wrong. She might want me, but she's a long way from falling in love.

Cara

"I think Nik has cold feet," I say.

It feels good to tell someone. Even if the someone — someones, rather — happen to be his cousins. Mala and Aesha are closest to Nikhil, and know him best. I hope they have some insight.

On the surface, everything is fine. But in the last two days, Nik has been weird and distant. When we're with other people, he's been perfect. Warm and charming in the way only he could be, attentive to a fault — my cousins are crushed he doesn't have any siblings.

When he picked out this gorgeous, perfect ring, and his reasons were so thoughtful, I felt seen. Understood. For just a moment, I thought: maybe. Maybe this marriage doesn't have to be a sham.

But since then, something's gone wrong between us, and I don't know how to fix it. Why is why I find myself confessing my worries in the middle of getting our dresses hemmed for my wedding — God, how am I having a wedding? — tomorrow. I need help figuring this out before I drive myself mad.

"Cold feet would make sense if he we were any other man,

Cara," Aesha tells me. She twists her hair on top of her head, checking out an updo with the neckline of this dress. Mala and she both look gorgeous in the stunning shade of turquoise that we picked. "But you know Nik. He's not like that. When he makes up his mind to do something, he commits one hundred percent."

"I do know what he's like. That's what makes this so hard," I say. "He's being... honorable. But the closer we get to the wedding, the more depressed he seems."

The seamstress finishes fixing our hems. After arranging for the dresses to be delivered to our suite, and putting away our high heels, we head back to the salon.

"Coco," Mala says, using my childhood nickname, "Listen up. You are a gem and any man would be lucky to marry you. I promise you: Nikhil is not depressed over this. I'd say this is the most relaxed I've ever seen him."

Aesha snorts. "Because he's getting laid for the first time in forever."

"Aesha! You did not just say that!" I sometimes forget how blunt she can be. Must be all that lawyering.

"Well he is, isn't he?"

My beet red face is answer enough. Far too amused, my friends cackle at my embarrassment.

Even if I wanted to deny that we're sleeping together, I wouldn't. Nik is by far the most amazing man I've ever been with. If I'd tried to design the perfect lover, it would be him. He takes his time, always makes sure I'm satisfied first — at least in that department, everything is perfect.

"I cannot believe you're sleeping with our cousin," Mala says, still laughing. "Normally, I would blot this out of my brain, because it's too gross to think about, but honestly: good for you two. As long as you have to be together, why not make the best of it?"

"That's the thing, Mala. Neither of us chose this, and I hate that." I pick a turquoise color for my toes. "What if he meets someone over the next year, and he isn't free to be with her because he's stuck with me?"

"Never gonna happen," Aesha states. She passes the same bottle of turquoise polish to Mala, who turns it over and nods.

"He's never been with anyone for very long. A few months, maybe, but nothing real serious. He's mostly been focused on his work."

"So you're telling me the man I'm about to commit a year of my life to doesn't even know how to be a boyfriend?" I'm flabbergasted. This thing spiraled out of control and it keeps getting worse.

"He's not an idiot, Cara." Aesha pats my hand. "Like I said, once Nik commits, he commits. You have nothing to worry about."

Except my job, which takes me away from home all the time. When my shiny new husband will be free to just do whatever — or whomever — he wants. What if he resents me for keeping him from finding the person he really wants to be with? Or what if he gets bored of me? I'm supposed to just live with that until this year is up?

Deciding to keep my worries to myself, I change the subject. The afternoon rushes by in a blur of good-natured teasing and relaxing beauty treatments. Afterward, we go back to our suites to get ready for the rehearsal dinner.

When I walk into our room, Nik is there. He's got a shirt half on, and I take a moment to admire him. Even though I've seen him naked a surprising number of times in the last week, I still can't get over the sight of him. He's beautiful.

This would all be easier if he weren't beautiful on the inside, too. Nik could've stuck to a lucrative practice in cardiology. Instead, he gave that up to be a nomad, spending the last five years of his medical career saving lives in places most people are afraid to go.

He catches my eye, and I blush a little.

"Good. You're back a little early." He stares at his reflection in the mirror, focusing on his tie. "We need to talk."

"Have those four words ever been the start of a conversation that turned out well?" I ask. He gives me half a smile. My desperate heart leaps at the sight. I'll take any sign that he doesn't hate me.

"I thought we should talk about where we're going to live when we get back to Portland. I assume my house is a better fit than your condo. Would you want to rent out your place for the year?"

I stare at him — in shock this time, rather than lust. Clearly, I'm an idiot. Getting through this rushed wedding has been my whole focus. Nik's, too, I assumed. The practicalities of what it means to get married, like where we're going to live, hadn't even occurred to me.

"I— um." I clear my throat, try to sound more confident. "I don't know. Do we have to live together?"

Nik raises an eyebrow. "Of course we don't. It's our choice. However, you know my family. We'd hear about it. Pretty sure yours would be confused, too."

"Shit." I head into the walk in closet and drop my sundress into the laundry. I hold up a blue and a green cocktail dress, trying to choose one for this evening.

For crying out loud. If I can't even decide a little thing like which dress to wear, how on earth am I going to figure out the logistics of married life?

"Ugh. This keeps getting more and more complicated," I mutter. Nik comes up behind me and rubs my shoulder. I immediately relax into his touch.

"It's just a year." He shrugs and points to the blue dress. I step into it. "We can do anything for a year. It's not as if this will be the rest of our lives."

But I want it to be.

The thought hits me like a bolt of lightning.

I've been avoiding the truth of this all week long. The reason I haven't fought harder to get out of this marriage? Is because it's the thing I want most of all.

I'm in love with Nikhil Shah, and I want to be his wife.

It's not just because I've been in love with him since I was eight. It's the man he is now. The one who helps me chose a dress for our engagement party. Who helps zip me into it with such care. Who makes sure I have my wrap, because the A/C in this town is always on full blast. The one who says, almost as an afterthought, "you look exquisite tonight" and offers me his arm.

This dinner is torture. Although I love and am so grateful for all of the relatives and friends who've come to town, and I'm having a great time with them, I need this to be over. All I want to do is go back to our suite and tell him I'm all in. This might all have started with a lie that Nik and I told to help our friends, but underneath it all, there's the inescapable truth: I'm in love with him. I hope that someday, he might feel something for me too. We already know we're compatible in a lot of ways — maybe this relationship doesn't need a time limit.

Two hours later, I grab my purse. We've put in our time. Maybe if we slip out the side door, no one will notice.

I search for Nik, and find him on the restaurant's balcony with Sean and Theo, Aesha's fiancé.

"...I don't know, guys. This is such a weird situation. We talked about moving in together, and she froze up. That's got to be a bad sign, right?"

"Aesha wouldn't even discuss it for a year," Theo replies.

"But you two had something already. You weren't thrust together by circumstances out of your control."

"But I've seen that video of you two, mate," Sean comments. "You get on like a house on fire. If I didn't know you weren't together before that hit the internet, I'd think you're the love story of the century."

"In front of the cameras, sure." Nik's voice sounds regretful. "We're great at faking it. But that's because we both know there's a lot at stake. Neither of us wants to be the one to cause a PR disaster for Cara's company or for my old employer.

"This fake engagement turning into a real wedding is the worst thing that could've happened."

I slap a hand over my mouth to keep from crying out. My pulse roars in my ears.

So much for that dream, then.

Even though my throat is dry, my pulse is racing and I can't think straight, it's a relief: I'd rather not hear how much the man I'm marrying tomorrow hates that we're getting married. I need to get out of here.

I say my goodbyes and leave the party, with a lot of good-natured ribbing about the wedding. It's easy enough to smile and laugh along, despite the fact that I'd rather be anywhere else.

It's fine. I'm fine. I can do this.

When Nik comes to bed, I pretend to be asleep. But I lie awake, staring at the ceiling, long after he kisses my forehead, and his breathing gets soft and even. It's too late to back out. I swore to him that I'd do this, and I will.

Still the irony of having to survive the next 365 days without letting on that I'm in love with my husband isn't lost on me.

I know it's the right thing to do. Too bad it hurts like hell.

Nik

Looks like our wedding day will be perfect.

We have the perfect weather. The perfect bride. And the perfect plan, thanks to my aunt and my future mother-in-law.

If only I weren't dreading this event with every fiber of my being.

I reach for Cara, but her side of the bed is cold. I frown. It's been less than a week, and I'm already cranky when she's gone. So much for my attempts at cool detachment. I'm just a lovesick idiot.

Opening my eyes, I see the note she left for me. She's planning to spend the day getting ready at Mala and Sean's. I'll see her at the ceremony.

I text Sean and Theo.

> Cara's ditched me to spend the day getting fussed over. What am I supposed to do all day?

THEO

> I'm headed to the gym. Come spot me?

Sean replies with an extremely rude bunch of emojis. I'm

188

impressed that Mister "I don't use the internet, I just build things on it" knows what all of those mean.

> DUDE. I will absolutely not be doing that. You need to wash your virtual mouth out with soap.

THEO

> Yeah, Sean. You text your mother with those hands?

SEAN

> I contain multitudes, gentlemen. But Nik: you'll be on display this entire day. Better to do it without all that built up pressure.

I snort. Becoming friends with my cousins' partners has been an unexpected bonus of leaving DWC and returning to Portland. They're pretty smart about most things. Nevertheless, I'll be skipping their advice today. I decide to go for a run instead.

I'm about a mile in when a trio of women flag me down. They're hovering around a fourth girl, a pale redhead with a face full of freckles, who's sitting in the grass with a pained expression on her face.

"Hey! You're Dr. Shah, right?" One girl asks. "You're marrying that girl from FortyFab?"

"I am," I confirm. "Let me take a look at your friend here. What happened?"

"Tripped over a rock," the redhead admits. She winces, squeezing the hand of a dark-haired woman with a sharp undercut as I palpate her ankle.

The dark-haired one frowns at the pain on her partner's face. "I am so, so sorry, Katie."

"Lex, don't apologize!" Katie orders. She turns to me to explain. "Lex is my girlfriend, and she did this really sweet thing. She convinced me we were going on this quick run, but when I got to this point in the trail, Jess and Vi were standing here with a huge banner that said "'Katie, will you marry me?'"

"Which would have been great —" Jess, or is it Vi? — throws in.

" — if it hadn't distracted her so much, she didn't see that rock in the path," the other one finishes.

"A for effort," I announce. "Not to mention a great story to tell in the future. How many people can say they literally fell for their fiancée in Vegas?"

As expected, they groan at my terrible dad joke. Lex helps Katie up. The way they lean on each other puts a lump in my throat. They don't even make eye contact. They just know they can depend on the other person to hold them up.

I want that.

"You'll need to get that ankle x-rayed, to be on the safe side, but my impression is that it's just a sprain."

"Thank you so much." Katie tucks her hair behind her ear. "I promise, we're gonna go get this done right now, but can we have a selfie?"

Geez. What is it with the selfies?

"Generally, I try to have a shirt on when I get posted on the internet," I protest, but they ask very politely, and I cave. As long as she gets that ankle seen right away afterwards, the few minutes it takes for a selfie can't hurt anything. Heck, I flatter myself that it might increase donations to DWC.

I wave as they head into the hotel, Katie and Lex supporting each other. If only I could have that with Cara. I sigh, smile still on my face, preparing to continue my run. Instead, I turn around and see the scowling face of my cousin Aesha.

"If you're done flirting with your fans, Dr. Shah?" One thing about my cousin: she sarcasms like nobody else. "We have a problem."

My heart pounds. "What's wrong?"

"Cara saw you with them, and now she won't stop crying."

"What? Why? She can't possibly think —"

"I don't know what she's thinking, and you don't either.

That's the problem. You need to fix this, or there's not going to be a wedding."

~

"Cara?" I call as I open the door. "It's Nik." I shiver when I enter the room. I'm still in my running shorts and trainers, and the AC is on full blast.

She's sitting at the make up table, and looks at me in vanity mirror. Mala's holding her hand. Cara's stopped crying, but her eyes are bright. She frowns when she sees me, matching my cousin's expression.

"You shouldn't be in here," Cara tells me. "Bad luck. Although we've had enough of that, and our marriage hasn't even started."

"Mala," I ask, "would you excuse us?"

My cousin looks at my face for a moment, deciding if she should leave her best friend to my tender mercies. She gives Cara's hand a squeeze, kisses her on the cheek, and murmurs that she'll be right outside. Mala crosses the room to me, a scowl on her face, identical to the one Aesha wore minutes ago.

To me, she says, "you know I love her as much as I love you, right?"

"Of course I do."

"Make this right, Nikhil. It's like my friend Ria says: Don't let your pride keep you from getting what you want."

"What — what do you mean?" I lick my lips and try not to let my nerves show.

"There's a reason I asked the two of you, specifically, to come on this trip with us." Mala looks at me with pity. "I thought being in a romantic setting would help you come to your senses and tell her how you feel."

"How — how did you know?"

The look she gives me clearly says I am the biggest dumbass in

Dumbassville. She doesn't even bother to answer my question. She just leaves the room, shaking her head and laughing.

Okay, I think. *So Mala knows.* That makes sense. We're close. We practically lived together. But that doesn't mean —

My pocket buzzes again and again. I pull out my phone.

"What is it?" Cara asks. "Did you go viral again for your selfie with the girl you helped?"

"No," I reply. "Mala told the cousin group chat that all this time, I thought no one knew how I felt about you. So far the replies are LOL, a laugh emoji, ROTFL..."

I hand her my phone. Cara watches the replies come in, her expression as startled as I feel.

"This one —" she clears her throat. "This one says *'I caught him doodling her name in his notebook when we were sixteen.'*"

"That would be Pinky," I admit, feeling heat creep up the back of my neck.

"And this one: *'Don't forget the truly dreadful poetry he wrote about her.'*"

"Wow. Arjun really threw me under the bus there."

"Nik," she breathes. "What — what does this mean?"

She looks... not appalled? Hopeful? I can work with that.

"When you saw me with those girls earlier—"

"I wasn't jealous," she says quickly. "Not in the usual way. But you were so gentle and kind and you seemed to actually... like them? The last couple of days, I haven't felt that from you."

So much for my plan. I thought I was protecting us both by maintaining some distance between us, but I hurt her. I take a deep breath. Mala and her friend are right. This isn't the time for pride. Honesty is more important.

"I liked you the moment we met, Cara. And I wanted you the second I understood what wanting meant.

"In all my life, there has never been a woman I wanted the way I want you."

"Don't," she whispers. Closing her eyes against the tears she's already starting to shed. "Don't tell me this. Don't make me hope."

Tenderly, I wipe a tear from her cheek.

"It's true, Cara mia," I confess.

Now that the hardest part is out of the way, I can't stop myself. "We've had the worst timing. We were either too young, one of us was in a relationship, or I was out of the country. I couldn't ask you to commit to me when I didn't even know if I'd survive.

"But one thing has always been true. I've wanted you for forever. Now I want you to be my forever."

"After I offered to pay for the ring," she argues, "you acted different. Colder. I thought the weight of what we were doing finally hit you, and you were freaking out."

"I freaked out because I was getting what I wanted — but you told me to be sensible. That we weren't getting married for the usual reasons. That sounded like you weren't interested in making this a real marriage. I didn't want to impose my feelings on you, since you didn't seem to return them."

"But last night, I heard you tell Sean and Theo that this fake engagement was the worst thing that could've happened."

"Did you hear the rest of what I said?"

She shakes her head no.

"I said it was the worst because it put so much pressure on us." I reach for her hand. "Do you remember that first night? When we kissed on the steps outside?"

"Yes." Her slightly breathless tone and flushed cheeks say more than her one word reply ever could.

"How did that feel?"

"Perfect, she replies. "Like something old and new at the same time. Full of possibilities."

"And how did it feel when our families showed up before we even got to explore what our relationship could look like? Before we could figure out what we wanted?"

"Terrifying."

"Cara, I hate that you got pressured into this. If I could take it back, I would. I should never have put you in this position."

"I wouldn't take it back," she says softly.

"Why is that?"

"Because if you hadn't, I would never have realized that you love me."

She reaches for me, and I gladly step into her arms. When our lips meet, it's not like a jolt of electricity or a flash of heat. Just the quiet, perfect knowledge that this is home. She is my home. She always has been. Always will be.

"I love you, Nik," she murmurs into my skin, between kisses. "I should've been brave enough to say so from the start."

"That would've required both of us to be different people," I argue. "And me not to freak out when you said the L word."

Cara considers it for a moment, then shrugs. "You might be right."

"I'm not a husband yet," I say, giving her a saucy look, "But I do recall telling you how much I like that phrase. I know there are no sweeter words in the English language."

"Oh, really?" Cara's bold expression matches the smug one I know is on my own face. "I bet I know some others."

When she whispers some of those filthy, wonderful words in my ear, it turns out she's right.

But the sweetest words of all are the ones I hear her say later, in front of our friends and family.

"I do."

My husband adjusts the intricately embroidered wrap on my shoulders and presses a light kiss to my eager mouth.

"You ready, love?" Nik asks. I take his arm, switching my bouquet of dahlias, rosemary and buttercups to my other hand, and nod. I'm so psyched for this.

We're back at Hotel D, in the same ballroom where we had our first dance, and so much has changed. In the six months since our wedding, Sean and Mala have confessed to their parents that they, too, got married while in Vegas. As predicted, there was much uproar on both sides of the pond, but when the Shahs and the Reids realized they'd have yet another wedding to celebrate, including a trip to Scotland to visit with Sean's family, the fuss died down pretty quickly. Personally, I think Aunt Meena is most excited about the prospect of Uncle Ravi in a kilt.

Nik and I stroll down the aisle to stand next to Mala and Sean. We've been best friends for our whole lives, Mala and me. The fact that me marrying Nik made us actual family feels like the sweetest bonus.

I look over at my husband. Turns out he did go viral for helping that nice girl with the injured ankle. The Travel Network were impressed. So much so, they offered him a job as a medical consultant. These days, he writes a column for them and appears on air in segments about handling medical emergencies while traveling. He also managed to get donations and free airtime for Doctors Who Care out of the deal.

While I'm impressed with my gorgeous spouse every day, seeing him perfectly polished in his tuxedo does things to me that I don't want to admit in public. I bite my lip, already planning for the moment we go home and I can get him out of it. Nik catches my eye and gives me a cocky smile. He knows exactly what I'm thinking, and I'm pretty sure he's got plans of his own. The heated promise in his eyes makes my pulse speed up.

But for now, we get to focus on our dearest friends.

The music starts, and we all turn around to watch Aesha walk down the aisle with Uncle Ravi on one side, and her son Riz on the other. She's gorgeous in her stunning purple and gold lehenga, a sheer embroidered wrap over her shoulder. The gold and pearl maang tikka in her hair shimmers in the light. Theo's face is the definition of smitten. His eyes shine with love and tenderness. He straightens his tie and pocket square — both purple, to match her gown — and stands confidently, waiting for his beloved.

When the three of them reach the front of the room, Theo shakes hands with Ravi and does an elaborate handshake with Riz. They sit down as Theo and Aesha join hands, and turn to face the judge performing the ceremony.

This service is brief, compared to the traditional Indian one they've already had. In their vows, Aesha assures him that she will always make room for his extensive collection of hair products, while Theo promises to keep her well-supplied with steak dinners. They both pledge to support Riz in his ambition to become the world's most famous tuba player. When the judge pronounces them married, they're in each other's arms before she can even finish saying "you may kiss the bride."

The reception is wonderful, too. It makes me flash back to the engagement party, all those months ago.

I still don't have my video camera. And there are still moments I wish I could capture, like Theo and Aesha competing in a Bollywood-style dance off. But this time, when Nik sees me across a crowded room, and we cross over to each other, and everyone else falls away, I ask for what I want. And when he takes me into one of those dark corners and has his way with me, I confirm that my princess fantasies don't hold a candle to being his in real life.

Thank you for reading Bet On Me!

Ready for more? Book 4, Burn For Me, featuring Jade and Nico, is now available!

Turn the page for further adventures in the world of Hotel D...

Want More?

Need more of the sexy, steamy world of Hotel D? Get the series prequel, featuring Ria and Drew, by joining my mailing list.

Is this second chance too good to be true?

As a successful lifestyle guru taking my business to the next level, I know about risk. Making a deal with the notoriously tough CEO of this exclusive hotel chain isn't that. Our companies are a great match.

But the former boss has left the building — and his replacement is Drew Connor, the man who broke my heart fifteen years ago. Drew's still sexy, still charming — but he's skeptical of my plans for our business. Personally, though? The heat in his eyes makes it clear he wants to pick up right where we left off.

Which means I've got two jobs now.

First, convince Drew to take the deal. Two, avoid getting involved again. Because letting him back into in my heart would be the biggest risk of all.

A Little Gratitude

Thank you for reading Hotel D! It means so much to me that you've spent time with the Shahs, their families and their partners.

A few shoutouts here, if you'll indulge me:

To my family, whose support and faith in me means everything.

To my friends, who are so generous with their time and affection. Special thanks to K.M.: this series would not exist without you.

And to you, dear reader, for allowing me to tell you my stories. There are so many more where these came from, and I can't wait to share them.

About the Author

Nika Stone spins sexy, steamy tales of mature romance from her home in the rainy Pacific Northwest. She loves tea, tequila and tacos — not necessarily in that order.

www.nikastonewrites.com

Also by Nika Stone

THE CARTERS

Burn For Me

Crash Into Me

Fall For Me

THE BRENNANS

Play With Me

HOTEL D STORIES

Wish For Me